Into Thin Air

Into Thin Air

A Novella
by Paul Vasey

Black Moss Press

BMP

©Copyright Paul Vasey 1994

Published by Black Moss Press in September 1994
at 2450 Byng Rd., Windsor, Ontario, N8W 3E8.
Black Moss Press books are distributed by Firefly Books,
250 Sparks Ave., Willowdale, Ontario.
All orders should be directed there.

Financial assistance toward publication has been provided
by the Department of Communications, The Canada Council
and The Ontario Arts Council.

This is a work of fiction. Any resemblance to actual events
or persons is entirely coincidental.
Cover art is by Greg Garand.

Canadian Cataloguing and Publication Data

Vasey, Paul
Into thin air

ISBN 0-88753-245-4

1. Title
PS8593.A78168 1994   C813 .54   C94-900398-0
PR9199.3.V38168   1994

For Marilyn, of course,
for Kirsten and Adam
and
for Absent Friends

1

"Right here is where they found her car." We were standing beneath the arching August maples and birches of a farm-field lane off The Anson Road, Aubrey Scott and I. The lane rose by a series of small inclines and plateaus to a crest about a quarter mile in from the road. It was bordered, east and west, by split-rail cedar fences, greyed by rain and sun, greened with moss. The fences were all but hidden, shrubs and weeds gone wild. If you were driving, the bushes would finger the sides of your car, weeds and grasses whisper against the undercarriage. If you were on a tractor you'd have to keep a forearm up. Scourge of branches.

Aubrey remembered precisely where his daughter's car had been found because of the gateless opening in the split-rail fence, an opening which gives access to the western field. A set of tracks, wide and deep, veered off in that direction. Just beyond the opening, the lane crested. In attempting to make this final rise the driver — Heather, whoever — had got the car stuck in the mud. It was beyond the fence opening and just shy of the crest the police had found the car. Aubrey toed the spot. Oxblood loafer.

Perfect spot to ditch a car. The only oversight on the part of those who'd done the ditching was, it had been night, third week of October. They'd forgotten about the falling of leaves. Hadn't considered the possibility people in the farmhouse across The Anson Road might still be up, might be watching Cool Hand Luke on the television which sat under the sill of the road-facing window in the front room; might notice the eerie dome of light in the woods across the way; might be curious enough, half an hour later, to pick up the receiver and dial.

What the constables had discovered just after three in the morning of October the 17th, a Saturday, was a 1968 Ford, grey, four-door, with its trunk open and its front doors open and its headlights on and its radio on and its ignition on but the engine stalled. The car was down to its rocker panels in mud. "They tried to jack it out. The jack was under the rear bumper when we got here. It'd been raining all day, all night. A heavy rain. The base of the jack was sunk right into the muck. The ground was that soft. Then I guess they pulled one of the rails off that fence." Aubrey nodded in the direction of the fence on our left. "And they tried to lever it out. But it's an old fence and the rail just broke." He stepped over to the side of the lane and looked in the vegetation. He leaned down and picked up the rail. "Here's half of it." Then he dropped the rail. Dusted his hands. "Then I guess they gave up."

I asked Aubrey if there'd been any signs of violence. Traces of blood, evidence of struggle, bits of his daughter's clothing. He shook his head. Shrugged. Frowned. "Nothing. And that's the strange thing. Her keys were in the ignition. Her purse was on the front seat. Her wallet was in it. I.D., cash and all."

It was on account of the wallet and the I.D. the cops had known whom to call. I asked Aubrey about the call, what it had been like, picking up the phone in the middle of the night. Cop's voice, skeleton of details. "I didn't know what to think." He shrugged, then tilted his head a little to the left and made a frowning gesture. "It just seemed strange that she'd be in trouble and not call. She'd always called before. Any spot of trouble." He looked at the place where the car had been, then down the lane toward The Anson Road. "I was concerned. Of course. But I wasn't certain she was in trouble. I mean apart from the trouble of getting the car stuck. At least for the first little while."

He fetched a pack of Rothmans from the pocket of his golf jacket. He pulled one half way out and offered it to me. Lit both. "I was puzzled. That's for sure." He exhaled and scratched his head with the fingers of the hand holding the cigarette. "But I didn't think anything bad had happened. I mean, there were no signs of violence. I figured they'd gone into town to get help. I kept looking back down to the road there." He nodded in the direction of The Anson Road. "I figured any minute they'd come back, while we were there, the cops and I. Maybe in a tow truck, or in another vehicle with people to help them get the car out. But of course, it didn't turn out that way."

I was going to ask him if the purse hadn't been the tip off. The purse and the wallet, I.D. and all. I asked, instead, what happened next. "There wasn't much we could do that night. The police had the car towed to town. They wanted to dust it for fingerprints. Have a better look at it in good light. After they left, I just sat in my car, down there on the road. I sat there all night. I kept thinking she'd come back." He looked at me and smiled. Wan smile. "At least I kept hoping she'd come back."

I asked him what he'd thought about as he'd sat there, rain drumming his car, waiting for his daughter, and dawn.

You're fishing, a question like that. But the editors eat up the answers you're likely to get.

"I remember I had a lot of happy memories, sitting there. Little moments. You have children now. You know the kind of thing. The times we went fishing. She loved fishing when she was a little girl. The trips we took. The birthday parties. The walks we took. The talks we had. Memories from those years when she was young, and we were close." He was silent for a moment or two. "Self defence, I guess." I thought maybe he'd elaborate. About some particular memory. Instead: "At first light, we began searching. The constables and I and some volunteers. We searched until dark. The fields. The lane. The woods at the top of the lane. As much ground as we could cover before the light failed."

That was just the beginning. "Over the last three years we've looked everywhere. Must've covered this ground a couple of dozen times." Aubrey made a sweeping gesture with his right hand. "We never found anything. But I just keep coming back. I was here three days ago. I can't seem to help myself. Can't seem to stay away. It's the only place I can go, outside my head, where I feel close to her." He shrugged, one of those apologetic shrugs. "Crazy, I know." He scuffed the earth with the edge of his sole. Left shoe. "I keep thinking that perhaps the next time I come out I'll find something I overlooked the times before. Something that'll identify who she was with." He scuffed the earth again. Right shoe. I found myself doing the same.

Three years of scuffing the earth, crossing and recrossing the fields of corn and wheat, three years of searching the scrubby woodlands at the head of the lane and the rocky outcroppings beyond those woods failed to reveal the slightest trace of his daughter. "It's as though she evaporated." He drew on his smoke and then dropped it. Stepped on it. Ground it into the earth. Exhaled. "It's the damndest thing, when you think about it." And there hadn't been a day during the past three years Aubrey Scott hadn't thought about it. "I've got to tell you, it was driving me crazy. I couldn't stand thinking she was out there. Somewhere. I had to do everything in my power to find her."

So. Aubrey Scott went to see a friend. The friend owns an advertising agency. Aubrey had asked about the cost of placing a full-page advertisement in the newspaper. Which newspaper, the friend had wanted to know. Every major newspaper in the country. The friend had pursed his lips and made a little whistling sound. "I think he thought I'd finally gone nuts." Aubrey smiled. The friend had to do a little checking. Aubrey had waited. The friend consulted rate books. Made some calls. Then he totalled it up on an adding machine. He read Aubrey the figure. Aubrey nodded. 'Go ahead.'

The advertisments feature a picture of Heather Scott. The date of her disappearance. The number to call if the reader has any scrap of information which might lead to her discovery and, in large red numerals, the amount Aubrey Scott was willing to pay for that scrap. One hundred thousand dollars.

The ad was a heart-tugger. It ran in our paper. Front section, back page. We carried a wire story on the front page, about the ad campaign. The headline read: 'Father's last desperate attempt to find his daughter'. The city editor dropped the paper on my desk. He'd circled the dateline. 'Isn't that the town you're from?' I told him it was. 'You know this guy?' I told him Aubrey Scott had been a golfing pal of my father's. 'You know the girl?' I told him I'd gone to school with her. 'How long will it take you to get up there?'

Six hours later I was sitting on the edge of the hammocked double bed, Room 6, The Pink Flamingo Motel, phone book on my lap. Aubrey Scott had been surprised to hear my voice, after all these years. I told him about seeing his ad in the paper in the city. 'Have you got any information about her? About Heather?' I told him why I was calling. That I'd come to do a story about him. I asked if I could come out and talk. He was about to sit down for supper. But I could come out about seven. If that was convenient.

It was nearly midnight when I left Aubrey's place and headed back to the motel. I was up until 3, thinking of Heather Scott. And Aubrey. And the car.

It was the first thing I'd noticed, pulling into the circular drive which leads to Aubrey Scott's hill-top home, the '68 Ford, grey, show-room, parked on an asphalt pad beside the three-car garage.

When we'd finished talking, Aubrey had shown me to the door. Followed me into the yard. We wound up talking in front of Heather's Ford. 'She loved that car. Well, of course, you know that. Her pride and joy. Washed it every weekend. Changed the oil every two thousand miles. If she comes walking down the lane one of these days I want it to be the first thing she sees. Runs like a top. I start it up every week or so and drive it up and down the lane.'

He opened the driver's door, slid behind the wheel. Put the key in the ignition. Turned it. The engine turned, but wouldn't start. He pumped the gas pedal a couple of times. Tried again. And again. 'I know it's not the gas. I just filled it up, a couple of months ago.' He pumped the pedal, turned the key. He'd flooded it. You could smell the gasoline. He pumped the pedal half a dozen times, then turned the key and held it. The starter turned and turned and turned. No dice. Aubrey Scott leaned out the open door. 'You go ahead. I don't want to keep you. I'll just keep trying until I get it started. Thanks again. For coming all this way.' Then he twisted the key and held it. Pumped the pedal. Furiously.

Two drinks later, Room 6, The Pink Flamingo, neon semaphoring, trucks huffing past, I rewound the tape of our conversation. The last bit. Played it through one more time. Aubrey's voice, weary and reed-thin: 'Sometimes, at night, I hear her calling to me. She seems to be very far away. Her voice is very faint. But it's her voice. She wants me to help her. And, of course, I can't. You can't imagine. You could never imagine.'

Then you hear the faint click of the recorder being shut off and, almost immediately, the sound of the recorder being turned on, then the sound of the engine of Heather Scott's car, turning and turning and failing to catch. A silence. Then Aubrey Scott pumping the accelerator. Then the engine turning and turning, failing to catch.

First thing this morning, before shaving, before showering, before looking for a smoke, I rewound the tape and played it back. And again. Then I called Aubrey. I asked him if he'd be good enough to meet me out at the laneway where they'd found Heather's car. He didn't hesitate. Didn't ask why. All he said was, it'd take him about half an hour. Maybe a little less. I told him I'd meet him by the side of the road. 'You know where it is?' I told him I knew exactly where it was. Then he remembered. 'Of course. I forgot.' Twenty-five minutes later, there he was.

We'd parked on the shoulder and walked in. He in one tire track, I in the other. Tractor and wagon ruts. Wide enough so you didn't have to put one foot directly in front of the other. Between the ruts there was a crown of grass and weeds, grown long.

Aubrey hadn't said a word on the way in. He'd kept his head down, as though looking for something he'd dropped, last time he'd come this way. He stopped when we reached the spot where his daughter's car had been discovered three years earlier. "Right here." Reedy voice. An old man's voice. Aubrey Scott was just past sixty. His cheeks were drawn and his skin, particularly around the eyes, was deeply lined. He was wirey. Though he was above six feet he looked shorter, on account of his stooped shoulders. He dressed expensively: loafers, knife-pressed trousers, golf shirt, golf jacket. A study in shades of beige and brown. What was left of his hair was brown, though gone grey at the temples. Hint of handsomeness.

I looked back toward The Anson Road. We had achieved an elevation of twenty feet. Across the road the land flattens out for the space of half a mile or so then descends by a series of rolling hills to the bay which blues away to the north.

On the crest of the hill there is a farmhouse. Typical of the township: storey and a half, red brick, back to the bay, front windows eyeing the road. There may be morning glories yet at one bay-facing corner of that house, rose bushes in beds all around the fieldstone foundations. If someone has had the inclination to care for them. To the east of the house there is an orchard. Used to be. To the west, a garage. West of that, a workshop. If you passed the garage and the shop, and walked to the corner of the field you would find a foundation. Fieldstones cemented into place. If you palmed the grass back you could probably still see where those stones were charred by the flames which consumed the barn thirty some years ago. When that barn went up, the ocre glow could be seen by farmers for miles about. There are some still living who will remember it vividly. 'Looked like the halo of hell itself.'

Looking down from where we stood, Aubrey and I, you see only gravel patches of the road, the peak of the farmhouse roof, cobalt glimmers of the sun-dancing bay in the space between leaves and branches. The vegetation was that thick.

I turned and looked at the spot where Heather's car had been found. Imagined the dome of light in the downpouring dark of that October night. Imagined the silhouetted forms around the car. Two at least. Maybe three. Imagined muffled voices, the whine of the tires spinning in mud. Sudden silence as the engine dies. The only sound the sound of rain on the sodden leaves on the rivering earth.

And then?

"Smoke?" This time I offered him one of mine. We were standing on the grassy crown between the ruts. I put my notebook in my pocket. And my pen. Our eyes met. "What do you think, Aubrey? Realistically."

"Realistically?" He looked down at the dirt and then out at the field and then down at The Anson Road. "Realistically, I'm not sure this will come to anything. I don't suppose I'm all that hopeful. After all. It's been nearly three years. Three years this fall. That's a long time. If she's still alive, she obviously doesn't want to be found. She may not look anything like her photograph, the one in the newspapers. Then again, if she's ... if it's clues we're looking for, you'd think they would have surfaced, sometime before this. But you never know, do you? Maybe someone who sees the ad will have seen her on the street. Or know her. Know where she's living. Or perhaps they'll remember her face, and remember seeing her that night, or remember someone talking about what occurred. Perhaps some little fact will jog loose in memory. Sometimes that's all it takes, isn't it? It's like one of those puzzles you work on and work on. And suddenly the piece is in your hand and you see exactly where it goes and the picture is complete. The missing piece of the puzzle." I told him three years was a long time. Memories fade. Memories fail. "It's a faint hope. I admit that." He looked right at me. "But a faint hope is better than no hope at all. You know what they say: 'better to light a candle than curse the darkness'. Those ads. They're my candle." Wan smile.

When we got back to the road he shook my hand. He thanked me for coming all this way to do a story. "Who knows? Maybe it'll be your story that does the trick." I told him I hoped it would. He got into his car and started the engine. "Will you send me a copy of your story?" I told him I would do that. He said goodbye. Closed the door. Turned in at the first lane, reversed, headed back the way he'd come. He waved as he drove slowly past. Same thin smile. I gave him a wave. Flick of the wrist. Nod and smile.

2

I leaned against the front fender of my car. Looked at the farmhouse, the garage, the workshop, the bay which was their backdrop. I was weighing the options. I swung one way, then the other. Get in the car, head back to town. Start making the rounds, familiar faces. Or, leave the car on the shoulder of the road, walk down the lane, knock on the farmhouse door.

Smoke number two. I have happy memories of that farmhouse. But not many. Make what you will of circularity: tragedy drew us to the place, drove us from it. A circle of flame. 'Nothing but sorrow grows from ashes.' So Mrs. Samson had thought, after the fact. Mrs. Samson, from down at the store. Perhaps. But it was Father she should have warned. Father wouldn't have given her the time of day. Her, or anyone else.

'It was a whim.' So said Father after he'd bought the place. 'I was driving out that way and happened to notice the sign.'

In fact, reading his Globe in The Harmony he'd overheard the talk about Abe Dixon's awful loss in the dead of that January night. There'd been nothing anyone could do, neither neighbours nor volunteers nor Abe himself, after rescuing half a dozen head of cattle and a few chickens and pigs, but to stand in the shin-deep snow under that vaulting star-spangled full-mooned sky, stand and watch the fire, speaking in tongues, showering sparks.

Such a loss is bad enough, for what is a barn but the heart of a farm. Worse yet for a man Abe Dixon's age. 'Broke his heart, that fire did.' People will tell you that, all these years later. 'His heart or his spirit or whatever it is you want to call it.'

That morning, crunching across the gravel where the fire had melted the snow away, skirting the still-smouldering ruins, Abe Dixon had climbed the slanted ridge of soot-blackened snow which the heat had melted and the night had turned to ice. Walked across the snow-duned field. Presented himself at the kitchen door of his neighbour. 'Looked like death, Abe did,' said Henry Hill. 'Grey and stubbled and vacant in the eyes. And he says 'Henry,' he says, 'you can have the land and the house and you can pay whatever you think is fair.'

Henry Hill says that he said he didn't need the house, or want it. As for the land, it was no time to be making decisions of the serious sort. 'But he says to me, 'Henry,' he says, 'the decision's been made for me.'

So Henry Hill had consented to buy the land, all but the two acres surrounding the house. That afternoon Jacob Johns had come out from town and hammered a sign to the trunk of one of the maples at the head of Abe's lane: For Sale, House, Orchard. Early that evening, all his earthlies packed into the snow-cornered bed of his half-ton Chev, Abe had driven to his sister's place in town.

Early that morning, some of the regulars in The Harmony had been out already, others were heading that way soon, to have a look. Father would have followed but for work to be done at The Plant. It was a little after lunch before he could get away. He made his way as far as Samson's store, the only directions he'd overheard. Credit where it's due, he'd not been about to ask. All he'd had to do from Samson's store was follow the procession.

Among these others, Father had driven out to see the ruins of Abe Dixon's barn just as he would have driven down to the harbour to see a fishing tug turtled at her moorings. It was a curiosity. Something to talk about, come supper.

Then he'd seen the sign Jacob Johns had nailed to the maple and he'd used that as a pretext for a closer look at the ruins and the blackened, crusted and bloated corpses of the cattle and the sheep and the horses. He'd crossed a line no town person, certainly no one from the township, would have dreamt of crossing. But it was a line Father neither sensed nor saw until too late. Until, turning from the ruins, he encountered Abe Dixon, suspendered, stockinged, standing on his side porch. Not knowing what else to say, but knowing something demanded saying, Father merely jerked his thumb toward the head of the lane. 'I've come about the house.'

'Bought the place for a song,' Father said. Once too often. It was his fate, it seems, to be last man in on these secrets of life lived beyond the city. He had said as much to Mother, by way of placating her I think. He'd said so again at the Rotary, by way of showing, as a city man will, he has come out best in any kind of dealing, particularly when he fears the opposite may have been the case.

But in the town, and certainly the township, no man would have dreamt of making such a boast. Each would have been at pains to explain with a suck on his pipe, a shaking of his head, how he'd been beaten in the deal. How he'd allowed his heart to rule his head. How he'd surely be more alert next time.

It was Father's misfortune to have made this boast to a man married to one of Abe Dixon's cousins. Word went out as word will: Father had bested Abe Dixon. Worse yet, he was gloating. This seemed to harden opinion against Father. Confirm in previous doubters the conviction he was just another shark, finning in shoal waters, quite capable and willing to take the legs off, above the knees, should the floundering flail into his path.

Henry Hill, on the other hand, Henry who said little at the best of times and nothing whatever on the subject of Abe Dixon's two hundred acres, Henry who let talk roam where talk will, Henry was seen as a good and Christian neighbour and friend, a man who had gone into the bank and into debt so as to buy land he didn't need, thus freeing his neighbour from the burden of living on land he could no longer tolerate seeing or working or walking. Henry Hill was a prince of a fellow, was Henry.

Truth be told, Father had paid the going rate for a house of that sort, in that sort of disrepair. And who but a city man would have bought the place at all, stripped of its land? A further truth: Henry Hill had not gone into debt at all. Never mind what Hurl Samson said his sister said, who worked at the bank and ought to have known. Henry had merely written a cheque. The cheque, as anyone could have seen for himself if he'd seen it, had been for thousands less than the land would have fetched had word of its sale been spread through the township giving rivals an opportunity to bid.

If they'd been playing poker, Henry Hill would have held his cards so close to the vest he'd have had to undo a button to finger one out. Father? Father's cards would have been reflected in his eyes, in the set of his mouth, as in a mirror.

What the hell.

Betty Beaton fingered the sheer curtain back from the window of her kitchen door. Squinted. Frowned. I told her my name. It took her a few seconds to put the name and the face together. Then she smiled and shook her head in an apologetic kind of way, and opened the door. "You haven't aged all that badly. I should have known you right away."

I told her I was sorry to startle her. She told me to come right in. "Never mind your shoes. Your shoes can't hurt this floor." Checkerboard of grey and black linoleum where once there'd been beige. Same cupboards, though the varnished doors had been sanded and painted not long ago. Same view of the white-capped bay framed by the window above the sink. "It's been a while, eh? Fifteen years?" I smiled. "More than twenty." "Fancy that."

She asked after Father, how he was doing these days. I told her he was doing about the same. "That's a shame. Really it is." She didn't seem to know where to take things from there. "Coffee? It won't take a minute. If you don't mind instant." I told her instant was fine. She nodded in the direction of the kitchen table in the centre of the room. "Have a chair."

She filled the kettle and took two mugs down from the cupboard to the left of the sink and set them on the table. "Milk?" I said that would be fine. She brought the plastic container from the fridge and set it on the placemat. "You want some cookies? A sandwich?" I told her I'd just finished breakfast.

She leaned against the counter, her back to the window, arms crossed. "Was that you up the lane?" I told her what had brought me home. She shook her head a couple of times. "I get shivers, even yet, thinking about that poor girl. And now Aubrey, with his advertisements." She shook her head again. "Isn't that sad?" She wondered whether I thought the advertisements would do any good. I told her I hoped they would. But I had my doubts. She said talk around town took the same track.

She put the jar of instant coffee in front of me, and a spoon. "Fix it how you like it. I'm always making it too weak or too strong." Then she poured the water. My mug. Hers. "Imagine. Something like that happening right across the field. Who'd ever have thought?" She returned the kettle to the stove, then sat opposite me. We stirred. The sound of chimes.

I asked her what they'd seen that night, she and Hugh. "Just the lights. It was eerie, eh? We were watching the late show and Hugh had got up to get us something to eat and he said 'Betty, have a look at that will you?' and I said 'Have a look at what?' and he said 'Have a look at the light. There's light up the lane.' You couldn't see the headlights, eh? on account of the car facing the other way. All you could see was a halo of light in the trees. That was all. Just the light. We couldn't see the car, of course, until we went up there. But there was no way we were going up there until after the police got here.

Of course that was later. At first, we just assumed it was a lover's lane type thing. Kids use it for that, eh? Kids still it use it for that, from up and down the line. But they don't leave their lights on. Last thing they want is someone knowing they're up there. So when the light was still there a little while later Hugh said 'Betty, I'm calling the cops'. He was all for going up there himself. Taking the gun and going and having a look-see. But I told him 'Hugh,' I said, 'you ain't taking no gun anywhere in the dead of night, getting yourself involved in who knows what'. And then I guess you know the rest."

I asked if they'd seen anyone leaving the lane that night. "We didn't see a soul. Course, it was raining. Dark as a cave. So there could've been someone that we didn't see. But we didn't see no one. It gives you the shivers thinking someone could have done something like that, and then walked away not three hundred yards from our own front door."

I asked what she meant. 'Something like that'. "Murder," she said. I asked if that was the opinion, around the township. "I don't think anyone doubts but she's dead." She frowned. "I mean, three years. Not a trace? She's gotta be dead, don't you think? I mean even Houdini couldn't disappear that completely, and still be alive." I shrugged. I told her stranger things had happened. "You think she could still be alive?" I told her people had been known to step out of one life and into another. I told her it happened all the time. "May be. But I wouldn't put my chip down on that square." She smiled. Then she wondered whether I wanted my mug refilled. I shook my head and stood. I told her I'd coffeed myself right out now. But I wondered if I could ask her a favour. "It's right over there. On the wall."

I told her I didn't need the phone. "I was wondering if you'd mind if I took a quick look through the place." She seemed surprised. "It's quite a mess. I haven't had a chance to make the bed." I told her I wouldn't mind the mess, or report it. She laughed. "Be my guest."

A few minutes later she shook my hand. She said it had been good to see me again. After all these years. She said for me to give her best to my father, next time I saw him. "It's a sorry thing about your father. Really. And him such a bright one." She shook her head. "Who's to account for turns like that, eh?" I told her that was the thing about life. It was all turns. Most of them unexpected. She said she had to agree.

I asked if she'd mind my walking around the property for a few minutes. "Be my guest."

The orchard had gone to ruin. It wasn't the Beatons fault. The orchard had gone to ruin long before they bought the place, and long before we'd bought the place. There was no telling when the orchard had last produced apples anyone could eat. Maybe when Abe Dixon's father still ran the place. Six rows by twenty. The ground was littered with windfall. Crow's delight. The air was heavy with the smell of rot. I walked through to the far end and stopped just short of the fence.

The farm due east belonged to Henry Hill. Or had. If he was still alive, Henry Hill would be in his 80s. Knowing Henry Hill, he'd be alive. And farming.

In the six years we lived on the place, Henry Hill had visited only once. The summer we'd moved out from town. The day after Mother had found the bone — sheep, maybe, or goat — on the low step of the front porch. Jawbone, teeth intact, flesh gnawed away, streaked with blood. Genius lay three feet distant, front paws crossed, tail drumming the earth, cockeyed smile.

'What's the matter with you?' Father had looked up from his cereal, and his book, when Mother had come into the room. 'Nothing.' Impossible, always, for Mother to conceal her emotions. They didn't show themselves in the obvious ways. Twitches. Tears. But a subtle shading and shaping of her features gave her away regardless. Anger or joy. Father had shrugged, more with eyebrows than shoulders. Went back to his food, his book.

Mother watched the car leave the lane and pass from view. She turned from the window and nodded toward the door. 'Come with me.' I followed her around to the front of the house where she knelt and swept away the earth from a spot near the porch. Turned, still kneeling, bone in her hand. 'Do you know what this is?' 'A bone,' I said. 'A jawbone, seems like.' 'This is a death warrant for that witless dog of yours. If your Father had found it, Genius would be on his way to the vet's right this moment. And if the farmer whose animal this was had seen him in the act, he'd have a bullet for a brain.'

'Good job you got that there dog chained.' It had been impossible, the following day, to read the look in Henry Hill's eyes. But I guessed he knew, or at least suspected, Genius had been involved.

'You let him run and you might never see him again.' 'Why would that be, Mister Hill?' Mother's eyes glittered. 'There's a pack of dogs, dozen at least, on the roam in the woods around here, Missus. Dozen at least. And if I catch them in my sights there'll be four or five fewer. They killed one of my sheep night before last. Chewed her right down to the wool and bone. It wasn't the first I've lost.'

'Can't something be done?' Henry Hill regarded Father, then Mother, then me. There was nothing to be done, except kill them. 'When something tame goes wild like that, and they were all pets, them dogs, one time or another, when they go wild it's like the madness. There's only one thing for it.'

He made a revolver of his hand, pointed finger, cocked thumb. Aimed at Father. 'Bang,' he said.

Mother had been right. Still and all it seemed a cruel paradox. Genius had had the run of the town. Now, a month later, surrounded by woods and fields, he was forced to spend his nights indoors and his days in that part of the yard he could reach, chain sliding along the clothesline Abe Dixon had strung from the hook by the front door to the elbow of an apple tree at the edge of the lawn.

Strange. Though he could have wandered an area twenty feet on either side of the clothesline, Genius chose instead to merely pace from the house to the tree and back. All summer he paced until he'd worn a track through the grass. Dusty in the heat. Puddled in the rain. Sometimes, just before turning back toward the house he'd pause for a moment. Ears pricked. As though he'd heard some kind of call from the bush on the far side of the road. He'd stand and listen and it appeared he might be about to answer that call. But he never would. He'd simply resume his pacing, up and back, up and back, like a soul tormented.

A little like that himself was Father, that first summer. 'You make more work than you do.'

Mother had smiled. But there'd been no smile in her voice. Father, passing through the parlour, had brushed against the corner of a doorway. A flap of wallpaper, crusted and faded, had caught his elbow. He tore a V of paper loose from the wall. For ten or fifteen minutes he pulled and ripped. Having reduced the wall to tatters and ruins, he bundled the paper and stuffed it in the kitchen garbage. Off he went, where ever it was he'd been heading when the wallpaper had caught his elbow and attention.

For two days, Mother and Martin and I, pail and sponges, had soaked down the walls and stripped the rest of the paper and finished the room, though finishing that particular room was not the job we'd been planning to do.

That was Father. Mother, too. For a job begun was a job in need of finishing. Once she started something, or once Father had started something for her, she was powerless to stop.

Not quite finished that room, just about finished the papering of the second wall, we heard him in the kitchen. Chip and crack. We found him on his knees, putty knife in hand, prying free those squares of linoleum which in their old age had struggled a corner free of their bonding. He'd removed a tile here and half a tile there and six or eight in front of the door and then dumped them in a cardboard box. Off he went.

'Damn that man.' Father was, all that first summer, a way I'd never seen him before. Jobs catching his fancy, but not his imagination. Nothing holding him. His mind skipping from thought to thought. 'Why don't you just sit and read a book for Heaven's sake? We'd be better off.' He'd tried that. But his books seemed to be calling him in a confusion of equal voices, none very compelling. Thoreau in the bathroom. Wordsworth by the bed. Rexroth in the workshop. Melville in the kitchen. All bookmarked in the early pages. None touched for days or weeks after the title had caught his eye. Mother finally gathered them up and returned them to their cartons where they would have to wait until Father built the promised shelves.

My memory of him from those summer days is of a man anxious to be where we were not. At the least hint — 'we'll have to get some more paint' — he'd be out the door. Next thing, we'd hear the engine starting, the transmission whining in reverse, gravel crunching under the white-walled weight of the Buick. Hours would pass. He'd return, often as not, without the item he'd gone to fetch. 'Damn. Forgot. I'll go right back and get it.' A fever of comings and goings.

'You might at least take the boys.' Father would look at Mother. Then at us. Then at her. 'They can come along if they wish.' Off he'd go, again and again, the least provocation, slightest excuse.

It was that summer, it seems to me now, the arguments began. Arguments which for the first time in my memory ended with the uttering of oaths, the slamming of doors. Even then I sensed those arguments had a hollow ring. Truth was: Father needed to break away. He'd take any excuse he was handed. Create one, otherwise.

What he thought about in those days we knew not. Where he went, he wouldn't say, we couldn't guess. If Mother pressed, which she did at first, he'd say, schoolboy style: 'out', 'just driving around'. Out and back. Out and back.

It was the latter part of September, third week of school, a Tuesday, that I walked up the lane and saw

Mother. She was sitting on the front stoop, cradling Genius. I called. Genius didn't move. I left the lane, crossed the lawn, called his name again. Slapped my thigh. Mother stared, still as stone, Genius dead in her lap. 'He strangled himself. Somehow. I don't know how. I found him hanging from the railing, the chain around his neck. The goddamn chain around his neck.'

We buried him, Mother and Martin and I, before Father came home. Between the last of the trees and the first of the fence posts, far eastern corner of the garden.

Take a spade, dig down a couple of feet, you'll find him. What remains of him. Just about exactly beneath my feet.

I scuffed the earth. Left foot. Right foot. I looked over at Henry Hill's place. Then turned 90 degrees to look at the woods which lay beyond The Anson Road. The opening to the farmer's lane.

I thought about what Betty Beaton had said, about the car in the lane. How she and Hugh had assumed it was a lover's lane type of thing. 'Kids use it for that, eh? Kids still use it for that, from up and down the line. But they don't leave their lights on. Last thing they want is someone knowing they're up there.'

I found myself thinking about coincidences, about the curious way life has of circling back on itself. I found myself thinking about windows rolled up against mosquitoes, windows slowly fogging, the warmth of a back against my chest, my groin, the smell and stiffness of newly-sprayed hair against my chin, the fuzzy feel of angora, the warm give of breasts beneath my palms, the sound of Heather sighing.

Into Thin Air

It used to surprise me when life threw you one of those curves. Used to. I'm getting harder to spook, the older I get. These days, the big surprise is when life doesn't circle around, sneak up from behind.
Still.

3

The last time I'd checked, the police detachment had been on the East Hill, beside the highway leading south out of town. But I hadn't checked in twenty-some years. I drove another mile and a half. Pulled in at Saul's wrecking yard. I asked one of the coverall kids about the detachment. When they'd moved it. He wasn't sure about me. Wasn't sure at all. 'Beats me, mac.' The detachment had been where it was now for as long as he could remember. From the looks of him, he'd have been born about the time I quit town.

The detachment is a single-storey, aluminum-sided affair beside the highway leading north out of town. I parked beside one of the cruisers in the side lot. A receptionist looked up when I came in. She smiled. Greeted me by name. I tried to fake it. "You don't remember me, do you?" I apologized. "You don't have to apologize. It happens all the time. Bonnie. Bonnie Nelson. Used to be." She held up her left hand. A band, no diamond. "I married Denny Symons." I asked how he was doing. I was trying to put a face to the name. He was doing fine. He owned his own garage. They had three kids. She asked about me. Was I married. Where was I living.

What was I doing. "What brings you back home?" I told her.

"Wasn't that a shame? About Heather?" Bonnie Nelson shook her head. "Not that it wasn't bound to happen, sooner or later. The way she carried on, eh? And who with. Still." I asked her what she meant. Carrying on. "You don't remember?" I remembered. What I wanted to know was what she knew. I shook my head. "Lousy memory."

"Well, let's just leave it to your imagination. You always had a pretty lively imagination." She smiled. I asked if the officer was still in town, the one who'd investigated Heather's disappearance. "Sure. He just came on shift." Bonnie Nelson stood and came over to the counter and opened the half-door so I could walk in. "Let's see if you remember him."

Last time I'd seen Willie Green he was a string-bean centre, six-two, hundred and fifty pounds, on our high-school basketball team. That was twelfth grade. A lot of years ago. Willie Green had the same dimpled smile. But he'd lost a lot of his curls and found some pounds since his days with the Falcons.

Bonnie Nelson shut the door on her way out. Willie Green, Sergeant Green, indicated a chair facing his desk. "Coffee?" I told him I'd had my fill for the day. Maybe the week. But I wouldn't mind a smoke. "Go right ahead." He pulled out a pack of his own. We were fifteen or twenty minutes talking about the old times before Willie Green scratched another match, looked past the end of his cigarette, wondered what had brought me back to the old home town. Back of Beyond was the way he referred to it. I told him about my visit with Aubrey Scott.

"Oh." I told him what kind of story I had in mind. He wondered what he could tell me that I didn't already know.

I told him I wanted to know about the ins and outs of the investigation. From the beginning. "You got a couple of weeks?" He smiled through a veil of smoke. Then he started. Just about where Aubrey had left off.

"We didn't know, at first, what we were looking for. A missing person. Or a body. Mister Scott didn't seem all that concerned. At least at the start. I couldn't get a read on him. I knew she'd done this kind of thing before, eh? She had a knack for disappearing. Couple of weeks. Couple of months. And Aubrey indicated, eh, that she was a bit of a free spirit. That's his words. I guess there's other ways of putting it. But he's her father, eh?"

Three days after the car had been found, Aubrey Scott got to worrying. "By then, of course, we'd lost three days. Three days when it did nothing but rain." By the time the cops got serious about looking, any trace of Heather Scott and her companion, or abductor, had seeped into the chanelled soil.

Willie Green and his superiors organized a search of the adjacent fields and of the woodlands at the head of the farmer's lane. "Have you been back in there?" I told him I hadn't been back in those woods since I was a kid. "Well, all they've done is grow since then, taller and thicker. Some places in there it's like a goddamned jungle. You need a chainsaw to get through. I'm not joking, neither." They'd taken dogs in. Organized searches with army cadets and boy scouts and all the volunteers they could muster. Made passes with helicopters. They'd made a grid, three miles by three miles. They covered the entire area once. The accessible parts, two times, three times. "We even had some cave crawlers come in and check out the crevices back there in the woods. Some of them crevices. Shit." He shook his head. "They go all the way to fucking China." It all came to the same thing. "Dick all."

For more than a year, Willie Green had done nothing else but follow one lead to another. He'd checked out everyone Heather Scott had been friends with. He'd checked out her former boyfriends, her former husband, her former lovers, all the people she hung out with. "I even went back to the yearbook. At one point I was going to have the boys down in the city check you out."

Then Willie Green had gone back to regular patrol work. Then he'd been promoted to sergeant. "For the last year and a bit, the file's been more or less inactive. Every once in a while we'll get a tip. Someone's seen her on Yonge Street, or in a bar in Montreal or on a beach in Vancouver. Now and then you'll get a tip that someone's overheard someone talking about someone else who heard who killed her. That kind of thing. I've followed them all right into the freezer."

I asked him if he was a betting man. "Once upon a time," he said. But he gave it up, once he figured out the nature of odds. I asked him where he'd place his bet, if he still did that kind of thing. He sighed. Drew breath, exhaled. "There are days I'd bet fifty bucks she was dead within five minutes of leaving that car." He shook his head. "Then there are days when I'd bet fifty she's still alive somewhere. Toronto. L.A. New York. Some place big. Some place a long way from here. Some place she can blend right into a brand new life. People do that, eh? They just want to disappear. Into thin air."

"Yes," I said. "Sometimes they do."

"Given her background, I'd say either one's a distinct possibility. And the truth is, I don't think we'll ever find out, one way or another. A gut hunch. But I really don't think so."

I asked what he meant about her background. "Close your notebook." A lot of what Willie Green told me in the next fifteen minutes came as no surprise. Some of it I remembered. Some of it I'd already guessed. The rest was inevitable. As he said at one point: "Someone seems to have cut her mooring lines." She'd been in a rock band when Willie and I were in school. A singer. Fair talent. Never have made it to The Top 10. But she was a hit on the bar circuit. Her kind of band, the drunker you get, the better they sound. Problem was, Heather was no better at judging herself than she'd ever been about judging others. When Janis Joplin popped up out of nowhere, Southern Comfort in hand, Heather Scott worked on the part. But the only parts she perfected were the drinking and the smoking and the partying. She and her band went on the road. The Outlaws they called themselves. One town to another. One bar to another. She never got to the big time. Never even the suburbs. But she wound up a long way from home. Then something gave out. Voice. Will. Spirit. Hope. Willie Green didn't know. One day, there she was, behind the counter in The Harmony. "She was as close to the bottom as you can get. All her friends were on the same rung. One up from the cellar floor."

Willie Green couldn't figure it. He wasn't alone. "Her coming from the kind of home she did. The kind of money. The kind of class. I mean, the coin lands the other way and she's sipping cocktails on the verandah out at the country club. Like her old man, her mother. Her sister." But as Willie was the first to acknowledge: "Sometimes things just don't figure, do they?"

I asked about the newspaper ads, whether Willie figured there was any chance that a hundred thousand bucks would pry loose the last piece of the puzzle. "The only thing a hundred thousand bucks'll do is lure every lizard out of every swamp from here to hell and gone." I asked him if he'd been seeing a lot of them. "We hired three part-timers, just to say hi to them on the phone." I asked him if anything remotely helpful had turned up. He shook his head. I asked him if anything was likely to. He looked at me for nearly a minute. Didn't even blink. Looked me straight in the eye. "You asking official? Or personal?"

Bonnie Nelson had a smile for me, on the way out. She asked after my Father. How he was getting along. I told her what I'd told Betty Beaton. "Do they think he'll ever get better? Ever get back to ..." I told her it was anybody's guess. I edged a little closer to the door. She asked about Martin, how he was doing. I told her he was fine, last time I'd heard.

What I didn't tell her was the last time I'd heard was twelve years ago. Twelve anyway. Collect call: "How's chances of wiring me down a little cash."

She asked where he'd gotten to. "Around the world. A couple of times."

"That's Martin. Never any moss on his stone." Yes, I said. That's Martin. She asked to be remembered to both of them. I said I'd be certain to do that. I shut the door behind me.

Hard as I tried, I couldn't detect the slightest familiar feature in her face. Or her voice. Could have sworn I'd never set eyes on her in my life.

"You asked him to what?" This was The Ex, over the phone. She'd wanted to know how Aubrey and I had wound up in the lane where his daughter's car had been found. So I told her.

I'd finished typing my notes from the interview with Willie Green and with Aubrey Scott. Then I'd poured myself a drink and tried to find some thread through what I'd learned, some narrative thread. I knew where to start. Where I was headed, I wasn't sure.

"How could you have?" I told her it'd been easy. I'd just asked. Actually, when we'd finished talking in his kitchen, when Aubrey and I had gone out to his drive, when he'd tried to get Heather's car going, I'd wanted to ask him. I knew I needed to get him out there, to have him in that spot where the car was found, where his story started. I knew that was the place where my story would start. The place where their lives intersected for the last time. I was on the verge of asking, while he was pumping the accelerator. Then I'd lost my nerve.

But there was no way I could go back to the city without going up that lane with Aubrey Scott. Without being there, and seeing what the place did to him.

"You're a ghoul." Suzie'd never have cut it in the trade. She'd be coming back with half a story every time someone sent her out on assignment. She told me once she'd rather have half a story than a guilty conscience. I told her I'd never wound up with either.

I told her I had to watch Aubrey walk up that lane. I had to walk beside him. Observe his face, his way of walking. Make note of the places where he stopped and what he said when he was standing there.

He'd told me all about the place, the night before. But telling isn't the same thing, though the telling was haunting enough. That's what had got me dialling the city. I'd played the interview back a couple of times, hello to goodbye. I needed an antidote. Another voice to block his out. For a few moments, anyway.

She asked me, Suzie did, about Aubrey's voice. About the quality of it which had bothered me. I told her of its reediness. Its weariness. I told her it was as though, no matter which topic he chose, Aubrey Scott would never have his heart in anything he was saying. It was as though something essential was missing from him. When the subject was his daughter he sounded so absolutely forlorn, so utterly lost, you wanted to put your arm around him. Give him a hug.

'Let me hear him.' I pushed the play button. Held the phone by the speaker.

Aubrey was talking about hearing Heather calling to him. About her wanting him to help her. Then the sound of the engine of Heather's car. I hit the stop button.

'Good luck, trying to get to sleep tonight.' We talked, Suzie and I, a few minutes more. She wondered when I'd be coming home. I told her I didn't know. I told her who I'd spoken to, so far. I told her who I was going to be talking with, tomorrow. I told her maybe I'd head out tomorrow night. The night after that for sure. I couldn't see it taking more than three days. Max. I asked her to put Ben on the phone.

It was Ben I was feeling bad about. I'd told him that I'd be picking him up tomorrow. Take him out for a pizza and a movie. Then things had changed in a hurry and I hadn't had time to call him, tell him I was leaving town.

Suzie said he'd just scooted out the door. Just as the phone was ringing, the door was closing. If she'd known it was me she'd have hollered. He was long gone now. "Tell him I'm sorry about tomorrow. Tell him I'll make it up to him when I get back. Tell him I'll call, as soon as I'm back in the city. Swing around, pick him up."

She said she'd do that. Then there we were, a gulf between us. Five seconds, ten. "So what do you do for an encore, Doctor Death? Snoop through graveyards? Visit the morgue?"

Very funny, I told her. She said she hoped I wasn't going to grease my hair back and don a cape and go out and bite someone in the neck. Then she giggled. Then she was gone.

There I was. All alone. Jug of whiskey. Tape of sorrow. Question: "What's the worst part, Aubrey?" Answer: "The worst part is at night." Long pause, during which a grandfather clock strikes the quarter hour. "During the day, of course, you can keep yourself occupied. In the garden. Doing errands. Being with friends." Another lengthy pause during which Aubrey lights a cigarette and then sips his coffee and then puts the mug back on the table. "But at night, you just lie there in your bed and you think how comfortable you are, with a house around you and a soft bed to lie in, and you wonder where she is and what's happened to her. You wonder if she's still alive. And if she's still alive, where she might be. What kind of life she's living. What kind of friends she has. If people are kind to her. Care for her. Or whether ..." Another pause. You can hear him walking across the kitchen to the counter, returning to the table. "More coffee?" The sound of coffee being poured. Aubrey's footsteps. Crossing, recrossing the floor. "And then, of course, you swing the other way. And you wonder what might have happened in that regard. If she..." Another pause, longer than the others. The pause ends with Aubrey clearing his throat and apologizing. "You wonder whether she suffered very long. And you hope, of course, that if someone did ... if she was ..." He clears his throat once more. "You hope that if she died, it was quick. And painless. As painless as possible. That's the very worst. That moment. Thinking about that moment. There's no way of explaining it to you. What it does to you. Thinking thoughts like that." Then you hear his lighter. You hear him exhaling. "And I hate winter. God, I hate winter. Those long nights when you hear the wind howling down around the house. When you see the snow whipping around. And you can imagine what the fields look like, out by the lane. The fields and the woods. And you know how cold it is out there, how bitterly cold. And I think sometimes that she's out there, somewhere. Unprotected. All alone. And there's nothing I can do to help her. Nothing at all. It's such a horrible helpless feeling. And as a father, you're not accustomed to it. You've spent all those years, all those growing-up years, kissing bruised knees and bandaging cut fingers and drying tears. You've always been there to hold her hand, to make sure her feet don't slip out from under her. To catch her, if they do. And then suddenly, when it matters most, you're unable to help. Absolutely powerless. It's just the very worst feeling you can imagine."

    We'd talked another few minutes after I'd shut the machine. Small talk. Acquaintances we shared. Events which had transpired since I'd left town. He saw me to the door. Then we went out by Heather's car. There was no way I was asking him about going out to the lane where her car'd been found. Not then.

I freshened my drink. Lit a smoke. Reversed the tape. Hit the play button.

The engine of Heather's car turned and whined. I don't know why I recorded that sound. I haven't the faintest idea. But it's just about the loneliest sound I've ever heard.

Lonelier yet: Aubrey's face, pale in the car's faint interior light. Aubrey's pale, determined, sorrowful face. Eyes fixed on the vanishing point. Foot pounding the accelerator. The engine whining and whining and failing to catch.

4

The Home is near the river. Not far from the centre of town. Half a block down, you're at Main Street. Hang a left, go three blocks, you're in the heart of town. Easy walk. But there won't be half a dozen residents who've made the trek. For them, a major outing is a walk to the corner and back. Good weather, they're on the benches in front of The Home. Staring at traffic. There's never much traffic.

I pushed out through the front door, came down the steps onto the walk. A gauntlet of eyes. I crossed the street, opened the door, slid behind the wheel, put the key in the ignition. They were staring at me now. The ones on the benches. The ones in the chairs on the closed-in porch, too.

I thought I recognized some of them, from the last visit. Year before last? Couldn't have been the year before last. Everything collapsing, all the turmoil: goodbye Suzie, goodbye Ben. The packing, the moving, the unpacking, getting settled. New life. So, the year before that. But maybe not. Maybe the year before that. Four years? I don't keep track. Which makes two of us.

I turned the key. Looked up to the second floor, third window from the left. I couldn't see him but I could picture him in his chair. I could hear the sounds of the place. Intercom voices, patients calling for a nurse, patients grumbling and cursing and laughing and moaning. Somewhere someone calling out 'Holy Mother of God. Holy Mother of God', telephones ringing, muzak in the background, feces and urine and disinfectant.

I put the car in gear. One of the grey-hairs waved. I waved back. She smiled. Waved again. I pulled out into the street.

End of the block, I turned right. I drove through Harrison Park. Down along the river, past the bandshell and the playground, the swimming pool and the tennis courts, around Lover's Lane and back out. On Main Street again, heading for the heart of town. Left here, right there. No particular destination in mind.

It's been years and years since I've driven the town like this. Aimless. Turning at whim. Stopping to appreciate whatever it is that arrests the eye. I'd forgotten how pretty the town is. Parts of it. How impressive so many of its buildings.

Visitors to the town almost always remark upon the beauty of the public buildings. The High School, a couple of the public schools, the churches, Town Hall, the banks, The Library, The Courthouse. I've seen townfolk stop when they overhear such remarks. Turn. Take a second look at the building which had caught the visitor's eye. Puzzled. The look they'd wear if a stranger remarked on an heirloom, long ignored on an upper shelf. They're hard-pressed to see the beauty. Heirloom, or public building. They don't see such things as much as they feel them. And what they feel in the presence of heirlooms, private and public, is solidity.

Fashioned of limestone quarried back of town, these buildings seem to have risen of their own accord from the earth itself, and to hold promise of enduring as long, precisely the effect desired.

In the city where I now live you'd have a tough time finding half a dozen such buildings. And yet, in town — the welcome signs, east and west, have never featured more than five figures — there must be thirty of these buildings. Maybe more. One, at least, at every major corner. All of them ringed and wreathed by trees nearly as old as they. When people say they are going to church, or the bank, or the library, they seem to capitalize the C, the B, the L.

The last time home I met a very old man on Main Street. A neighbour, once. Told me, at length, about a robbery which had occurred in a town down the road. He had memorized all the horrible details. 'It's gettin' closer all the time.' It may well be. But in some peculiar way, these old buildings of ours, and the institutions they house and represent, seem to be holding 'it' at bay. For the time.

When we moved from the city to the town we bought a sprawling once-proud home at the top of the Tenth Street Hill. It shied from view behind chestnuts and oaks, maples and elms, hedges and shrubs gone wild. If you elbowed your way through the underbrush you were looking down upon the town. In the distance, the glinting bay. At night, captivating: the bay was a wedge of darkness driven into the light-flickering heart of the town.

Directly below our house was the high school. Across the road a baseball diamond. Beyond the diamond, the Anglican Church. St. George's.

It had been Mother's notion, Father in his final revolt against organized religion, that I go down the hill and join the youth group. 'You'll make some new friends.' So, down the hill in the dusk I went, down the hill and across the diamond and tried the front doors. My knocking echoed, went unanswered. The side doors were locked as well. Ear to varnished wood, I could hear voices beyond the rear door. I rapped. Rapped again. The doorway was suddenly full of light. Two boys, silhouetted, stood above and before me.

The first punch caught me on the side of the head. Knocked me off balance, off the step. Then they were upon me. I was a minute or two, rolling and scrambling from their boots and blows. I didn't stop running until I was across the diamond, across the road.

'Well.' Mother had towelled my cuts. Father, behind her, spoke not so much to me as to her. 'Give me a pack of wolves any day to your pack of Christian lambs.'

Plead and implore as I might and did, Father had insisted on marching right back down the hill. 'You don't stand up to them now, you're as good as finished in this town. And you aren't even started.'

So once more I stood on the step, looking up into the light of the church hall. I recall precisely the stooped shoulders of my attackers. The soothing apologetic tone of the priest. The increasingly angry and violent voice of my Father. Spurning apologies, Father issued a threat of his own: lay your hands on my son, any of you pimply little bastards, and I'll have your balls for bookends. And if the priest knew what was good for him he'd put a collar, metaphorical or otherwise, on the pack of jackals in his charge.

On the way back up the hill Father had railed on about hypocrisy and treachery and betrayal and how it was one of the world's sad ironies and truths that things were not always what they seemed to be, neither as sure nor as safe. 'The greatest betrayals in the history of man have come at the hands of man's dearest comrades. Judas was neither the first nor the last of his kind. Bear it in mind. And great surprises will come raging out at you, as you have just learned, from the most apparently benign of doorways. The banks can break you. The schools mislead you. The courts wrongly convict you. The goddamn churches condemn and persecute you. Let it be a lesson you don't soon forget.'

His own lesson had come not four years later. It was October. Our third year on the farm. The leaves had changed. Some trees were bare. The air was chilled, even when the sky was clear, the sun shining. The school bus stopped outside Hurl Samson's store. Martin and I had gone in, asking for our mail. 'Your father's already picked it up.' Martin looked at me. I at Hurl. Hurl turned his palms up. 'Come in coupla hours ago, just after dinner.'

Father never came home in the afternoon. Rarely came home before supper was on the table. Lately The Plant had been working extra shifts to get the orders out. Father started early, was gone by the time we woke up. Stayed late, to supervise the shift change, talk with the night foreman, take a final tour around The Plant.

Father was in one of the fan-backed broad-armed chairs on the side porch. He had a cigarette in one hand, a drink in the other. We said hello. He looked at us. Nodded. Kept silent.

Martin dropped his schoolbag on the floor just inside the door. Kicked off his shoes. Looked at Mother. Jerked a thumb over his shoulder. 'What's with him?'

'The Plant's been sold. He's been let go.' I have often wondered at the cause of things. Wondered why things turned out for us the way they did. Wondering, I wind up, as often as not, in the kitchen that day, looking out the window at Father, seeing him in profile, smoking and drinking. Lost in thought. Utterly lost.

Pivotal moment. But there were others. Last winter, in the city, there was a storm. Rain turned to sleet turning the street and sidewalks slick and grey. I was walking hand in hand with my son. His feet flashed out from under him. There he was, hanging from my hand. 'Slippery,' was all he said. 'I almost fell myself. Earlier. Down by the corner. On my way over to see you. Hit a patch of ice and all of a sudden my legs and arms were like those circles in the cartoons.' Ben had looked up at me. Confused. 'I can't imagine you falling.'

'Never sick a day in my life.' Father's boast echoes down through the years. True, so far as I knew at the time. He was a robust man, strapping and muscled, his physical strength belying a lifetime spent in a chair in an office, one plant or another. If I imagined him dying, I imagined it only as a sudden soundless fall. Now you see him. Now you don't. Illness could be no match for him. Only Death could claim him.

And then one morning, the year before The Firing, our second in the country, late summer, edge in the air, first leaves turning, he failed to rise. Mother had called once, putting the bacon in the pan. Again, when the eggs were all but done. 'Go rouse your Father. Tell him his breakast'll be getting cold.'

He was on his side, knees drawn to chest. Tears clung to the tips of his lashes.

It was my first conscious moment of fear. Four days in the hospital and the pain in his head finally subsided. After fearing the worst, stroke, aneurysm, Doctor Brewer diagnosed nothing more than a sinus infection. 'Worst he's ever seen.'

Though better, Father seemed ill at ease. Bewildered. As a man will when he loses hold of something upon which he'd been certain he'd had a firm grip. 'Never sick a day in my life.' No boast now.

On the day he was to be released, I went to the hospital. Found him sitting up, neither combed nor shaved. 'The brush and bowl are there.' He indicated, with a nod, the top drawer of the bureau beside the bed. It wasn't until I fetched them out and placed them before him on the roll-away table that I realized he intended I should shave him.

I am still somehow strangely repulsed by the thought of lathering his face and then scraping it smooth, towelling it dry, Father all the while looking straight ahead, into distant space.

His listlessness, his spiritlessness, seemed to presage something more terrible than death, seemed to indicate that all the rules by which we had lived til then had, in the space of four days, been altered in some significant way, beyond understanding.

I was suspended between fascination and revulsion, razor in my young hand.

And yet today, sitting on the edge of his bed, looking at him, his pajama shirt stained with the leavings of breakfast, eyes dull, sunken cheeks stubbled, hair unwashed and spiked, shoulders rounded, my first impulse was to get his bowl and brush, lather him, shave him, wipe away the traces of soap, nose and ears. Get his pearl-backed matching brushes and set his silvering hair to rights. Present to the world, nurses and orderlies, patients and visitors, the face I know. Or remember.

I asked him if he wanted me to shave him. He was silent. Has been sitting, silent, by the window of one institution or another, now, for twenty-some years. Quietly burrowing deeper and deeper within himself. Finally darting down some spiralling path. Vanishing from sight.

Whether he hears, or arranges what he hears into some kind of sense and order, is beyond my knowing. Every now and then I think he almost turns to look at me. Forgetting himself. I've wondered whether, as I've headed for the door, he hasn't glanced at me out of the corner of his eye. I've turned. But, always, he's been just as he was when I'd turned my back on him, headed for the door. Stubbled and vacant as a fallow field.

"I was out at the house today. The country house." Father focused on the window pane, focused with great determination it seemed to me. As though by sheer effort of will he might will himself into flight, will himself through the casement and out of The Home and out of the town, effecting a soft and graceful landing in some place far far away.

"I don't know whether you remember Aubrey Scott. I'm up here to do a ..."

I told him about my visit with Aubrey the night before, and again this morning, out in the lane. Told him about my visit with Mrs. Beaton. "Do you remember her? She and Hugh, they're the ones who bought the place after ..." I told her Betty Beaton had wished to be remembered. As had Aubrey Scott. As had Bonnie Nelson. I talked on.

Suzie has asked why I bother. 'It's like talking to a post.' I tell her it's easier talking with him now than it ever was when he was alive.

'Talk to your Father', 'Ask your Father', 'Tell your Father'. Mother sometimes pushed me, physically, into the room where Father was to be found. I remember long and awkward silences, standing in doorways, waiting to be acknowledged. He would glance at me, over the tops of his glasses, as he might at a stranger. I'd begin. Ordinary tales of ordinary days. He'd look down. Lick the tip of his middle finger. Turn the page.

I gave it up. I'd have been twelve at the time. Twelve or thirteen. From that day onward, for the most part, we communicated with nods and grunts, partial sentences, single words except on the rarest of occasions. A truce of silence.

Suzie: 'It's like the sound of one hand clapping. You sitting there, talking away. For years, you didn't do much more than say hello to him, if that. Now?' This was years ago. After we were first married. I hadn't wanted her to come along. But she'd insisted. 'Look at the father, know the son.' I told her there were some things it was better not seeing, better not knowing. She said she'd be the judge of that. She'd stayed in the doorway. I'd sat on the bed. Talking.

It was on the sidewalk, on the way to the car, that she'd started doing all the wondering. 'I didn't know better, I'd say you were trying to get even with him. Talk his ear off now that he can't do anything to shut you up.' I told her what the world didn't need was another five-cent psychologist.

I stood up. Smoothed the bedding. "Better be going. Got a couple more people to talk with, before

I hit the road." I put my hand on his shoulder. He didn't move, or react in any way. He just stared at the windowpane.

"I'll be seeing you." Halfway to the door I looked over my shoulder. He hadn't moved.

5

There are pivotal moments in the history of every family. In ours, as in others, several. The buying of Abe Dixon's house. The buying of The Boat. Both came to represent a kind of fork in our familial road. Father had done the choosing, in both instances. Veering off, neither notice nor warning, from the well-trod and familiar road onto paths successively narrower and more treacherous. We could not have known how significant these turnings would prove to be. We did have our fears. And we understood this: the landscape beyond these forks was vaguely threatening, intimidating, to all of us except Father. This, as well: our equilibrium had been altered. We had a tougher time maintaining our balance as a family, as individuals. These two events entered our vocabulary, and changed it. We referred to our lives as having distinct phases with these events marking ending and beginning. Before The Move. After The Move. Before The Boat. After The Boat. More than simply moments in time.

The Boat entered our lives during our second summer in the country. After supper, Father had pushed his chair back and stood at the head of the dining room table. Wiped the corners of his mouth with his napkin. Laid the napkin on his plate. 'Into the car everyone. I've something to show you.' Half an hour later we were standing on the edge of the wharf at Nails McPhee's Marine Works.

The Boat lay at her moorings, a little low in the water and listing toward the wharf. Grand though she'd undoubtedly been in her prime and time, she was a weary old thing by then, weary and ill-used and worn.

A double-ender, forty-eight feet from bowsprit to rudder, she was an ocean going cutter. The building of her had been the talk of the town for years and years. Launched a quarter century earlier, she was born in the mind and at the hands of Doc Forster. He had been a neurosurgeon. More than a promising one. Then, trimming branches in a tree in his yard he reached a few inches too far. Trying to save himself, he'd succeeded only in driving the bone of his upper arm through its shoulder socket. Shattered almost every bone in his right hand. According to the talk, he could not abide the thought of living in the shadow of his former glory. So he left the city, moved to town, set up a general practice.

The harbour is ringed by warehouses. Remnants of an era when it was the commercial heart of the town. But even then, years before we moved up from the city ourselves, the railway and the highway had changed the old patterns. The warehouses, a good many, were long abandoned. Every year or two another would be reduced to ashes.

Doc Forster rented a warehouse down near the elevators. Ordered the foundry to pour him a lead keel. The crane deposited it in the yard and Doc hired twenty men to winch and muscle it indoors and set it upon a cradle, spine of his dream.

He worked on his boat nine years. He was very nearly finished it when, reaching for a hammer on the scaffolding which ringed the vessel, he reached once again beyond his grasp. It was his wife who found him, late that same night, in a pool of his own blackened blood on the concrete floor.

Every now and then you will hear about a car, almost new, neither scratch nor dent, which no one can sell at any price. It is said someone died in it. They say you can never get the stench out of the upholstery. More than that, a kind of curse attaches itself to such cars. You will hear stories, contradiction conveniently ignored, about unsuspecting buyers of such cars. Men normal as spring runoff being found dead themselves, slumped over the wheel, a hose fed through the vent window.

For such reasons, perhaps, no buyer could be found for Doc Forster's boat. No buyer from town, at any rate. Or the country around. But the summer following his death his widow took out an advertisement in the yachting magazines. Estate Sale. Presently The Boat was craned onto a flatbed and trucked down the road to Nails McPhee's Marine Works and there she was launched. Dark prophesies notwithstanding.

The Bay has many sounds and inlets and at the head of each there is a town like ours sprung up around and sustained by a deep and natural harbour. Twenty miles further north, a good day's sail from our town with a fair west wind, the new owner moored her not far from his cottage. For twenty years he sailed her and she was the talk of all who happened to catch sight of her out in the Bay, so grand she was, so fetching and fleet.

People in that town, and in our own, were waiting for some evil or disaster to befall him. But he died in his bed one weekend in the city. His sons argued over his estate and the boat remained in its cradle on the shore for the six years the courts required to settle all claims. By the time the victorious son launched his prize, dry rot had long since claimed what he had had such difficulty claiming himself. She sank like a stone.

What she needed was replanking. What the son could afford was simply enough patchwork to keep her afloat until someone might come along and notice the sign wired to the rigging.

'Isn't she lovely?' 'Other adjectives come to mind.' But Mother must have known it was too late, by then, for argument or appeal.

Two days later, Nails McPhee at the wheel, the tractor trailer laboured up the Linden Hill, dust-plumed its way along The Anson Road, grunted down our lane. The mobile crane, Nails' son at the levers, whined and winched The Boat free, swung her up and out and settled her, creaking and complaining, into the cradle beside the remains of Abe Dixon's barn.

Nails is dead now. The marine works long gone. In its place you'll find the parking lot and fenced pool of a bay-side condominium. In Unit 22 you'll find Marilyn Scott. Aubrey's estranged wife. She hadn't changed a whole lot in twenty years. Still blonde. Still trim. A few more wrinkles. She smiled and shook my hand. She said she'd had a change of heart. She'd told me on the phone to come to her place. She'd said we could have coffee and talk there. But now she said she felt like talking elsewhere. She gave me directions to the restaurant she'd decided on. She told me to go ahead, that she'd meet me there. Twenty minutes. No more than half an hour. She had a couple of things to tidy up.

A couple more things, apparently, than she'd counted on. I'd been sitting more than forty minutes in the booth at Sully's Restaurant when she walked in the door. Another ten minutes, I was going to phone her place. I wasn't expecting an answer. She was apologetic. She'd been about to open the door to leave when the phone rang. It'd taken her ten minutes to get off the phone.

It was one question after another, the first few minutes. She wanted to know how things had been going in my life. How things were in the city. Whether I was married. Did I have any kids. Did I ever see my Father. Had he improved in any way. Twenty minutes later, I pulled the tape recorder out of my briefcase. I set it on the table between us. She looked at it for a moment, then looked up at me. She breathed in deeply, the way a swimmer will before diving into the pool. She exhaled. Then she lit another smoke. She wondered where I wanted her to start.

I told her the beginning was as good a place as any. "The first year, I think Heather's disappearance drew us together, Aubrey and me. And Sandra as well. As a storm will do, when everyone chips in and does what can be done to ensure survival. You read about that, don't you." Her conversation was marked by long pauses, during which she sipped her coffee, or toyed with her cigarette, rolling the end of it in the ashtray. It was as though she was gathering her thoughts, ordering them in some way, trying to make connections of some kind.

"I do believe if her body had been found, if we'd discovered, for certain, what had happened to her, it would have been better for all of us." She had been looking down, speaking softly. Then she looked up. "It sounds dreadful, I know. But it's the truth.

"There were all kinds of tensions building. In all of us. And between us. It was horrible for Sandra, particularly. There was such an age gap between them. She was so young. Only nineteen when Heather went missing. It was only natural that she would want to do the things that teen-agers want to do: go to dances, go to parties, go out on dates. She refused, as often as not. Despite our prodding, despite our telling her it was perfectly all right. And when she did go, when she went out and had a wonderful time, she came home feeling worse than ever, plagued by guilt. Regardless of what we said, to assuage her.

"And then, and I know it makes no sense at all, if we succeeded in getting her to go out, Aubrey and I would be at our wits ends until she came home. Particularly if she went out in a car. We tried, I know I did, not to let her sense it. But now and then, some little thing we'd say would tip our hand. And she would fly into a rage — who could blame her? — and accuse us of trying to smother her. And she was right, of course."

We ordered more coffee and lit cigarettes and sat, for a moment or two, without talking.

"As for Aubrey and me." She looked at me and then at her coffee, stirred it, tapped the spoon against the mug's lip, set it down on the paper napkin, upside down, moved it until it was parallel to the napkin's edge. Looked up. "Heather's absence became a space between us. That's the best way I can describe it. A kind of gulf. I'm sure we both felt the same way, and there's no way I can adequately describe it for you. The cliches don't do it justice: an ache, a longing, a dull pain. It's all of that. But it's so much more. You'd have to be a poet to put it into words, I guess.

"You'd go to bed at night and she'd be the last thought in your mind. And you'd wake and she'd be the first thought in your mind. And your dreams would be filled with her, the vision of her. Scenes from your life which centred upon her. Surreal images: Heather drifting in and out of distant woods; Heather on the seashore, so far ahead you couldn't make yourself heard; Heather in a crowd as you passed by in a bus. All kinds of dreadful forlorn images. You can't imagine how helpless dreams can make you feel. Or how exhausted they leave you.

"At first, we talked about it. Talked endlessly. As though talking it through would somehow make it less difficult to endure. It didn't work. I don't suppose it can ever work. We talked in circles and always came back to the same spot: the void into which she'd disappeared. Nothing changed. Because, of course, nothing could change.

"And then we began to lose patience with each other. Began to chafe when the other raised the issue. And so we talked less." She looked at me over the rim of her mug, then set it down and looked at it. "Didn't think any less, of course." She looked up. "Just talked less. Gradually. And gradually we found ourselves on either side of a silence. And the silence grew, as silences do." She made the slightest shrugging gesture, and frowned. "And there we were. Stranded on either side of it."

She lifted her purse from the seat beside her and put it on her lap, opened it, pulled out a fresh pack of cigarettes, set them on the table and returned the purse to the seat beside her. She removed the cellophane and the foil and drew out a cigarette. "One of mine?" I accepted it, lit both.

"I know this is going to sound terrible." She looked at me, directly. "Because it is terrible. But I came to resent Aubrey. I developed a very real anger toward him. I came to loathe the sight of him, moping around the house, standing at the windows, staring out. Everything about him — his stooped shoulders, his voice, his vacant eyes — irritated me beyond words. It wasn't fair. It certainly wasn't just. But it was visceral. And there was nothing I could do about it. It was pure emotion and I was helpless in the face of it." She stubbed her cigarette and, almost immediately, drew another from the pack and lit it. "I came to loathe him. I couldn't stand to be in the room with him. I hated him.

"I wanted to get on with my life. This is two years, now, after the fact. I'd mourned myself out. And I'd come to this: all the mourning in the world, all the moping and all the talking, all the regrets and sorrows in the world weren't going to bring her back from where ever she was. I just finally felt I had to get on with my life. What was left of it. We're not young. Life is short enough, as it is. And I wanted to start living again. It's the best way I can describe it. I just wanted to live. I wanted to laugh again, and to enjoy things again. I wanted to get out of that terrible musty air of sorrow and loss and breathe the fresh air and walk in the sunshine and leave regret behind.

"I wanted Aubrey to let go, too. To leave it behind. To get on with his life. Our life. But Aubrey wanted no part of it, resented it when I told him how I felt, resented me. He once accused me of not caring, of not loving Heather." She looked at me, eyes wide. "Of not loving her." She shook her head. "It was right then, at that moment, that I realized I hated him. How it had happened, when it had started, I can't tell you. But when those words issued from his lips, I knew it as certainly as I've known anything in my life. I hated that sonofabitch. And then, of course, it was only a matter of arranging the details — renting a place, moving my things out of the house and into the new place. So endeth a life." She smiled. Wan smile. "Part of a life, at any rate. The old life.

"That's not quite true, of course. It wasn't all as clear cut as that. Not about the hating. That was cut and dried. But you can't walk out on your life without feeling all kinds of uncertainties, all kinds of doubts and regrets. Not regrets, I guess, as much as sorrow. A longing for things as they'd been. Even though I knew with certainty that those things were all in the past tense, irrevocably. Still . . ."

She finished her coffee and pushed the mug toward the edge of the table. She butted her cigarette and folded her hands.

"It was strange, those last few days before I left. I found myself looking for some sign that I was doing the right thing. That I wasn't just being impetuous. I wanted to be certain, somehow, that I'd leave with no regrets. That I wouldn't find myself a month down the road, or a year down the road, realizing I'd just made more of a mess of things than otherwise.

"One night I woke up suddenly. You know how you do? Your heart pounding. Thoughts whirring. Not knowing where I was. Or what time it was. Or what day it was. I was just suddenly wide awake, sitting up in bed.

"The sheet was thrown back on Aubrey's side of the bed. His robe was gone from the chair in the corner, and his slippers. I put on my own robe and went downstairs. There was a draft. This was

November. The air was bone-cold on my shins and ankles. A door open, somewhere. The kitchen door, as it turned out. Wide open. I'd just come into the kitchen from the dining room when I heard his voice. Thin, distant. He was out there in the yard, with a flashlight, a flashlight in his hand, his robe flapping in the wind, slippering his way through the snow, calling her name. Over and over and over. 'Heather? Heather? Heather?'

Blue eyes brimmed. She shook her head. "That was the day I left. Packed and went. That very morning." She knuckled her eyes. "I'd never felt such an urgent need to save my own life. That's the only way I can explain it."

Marilyn Scott put her cigarettes into her purse, snapped the purse closed, set it on the table.

"Thinking back, I should have been able to see the turning point. That moment when I might have helped. But he turned the corner before I was aware he was anywhere near it. Disappeared. By the time I got there, he was gone, lost to view. As you read, sometimes, in a mystery." She'd looked at me. "You know what I mean?"

I'd told her I did. She smiled. And apologized. "Of course you do. I'm sorry." I told her there was nothing to apologize for. She tapped a fingernail against the tape recorder which sat between us. "So. There you have it. Make of it what you will." She slid to the end of the bench and stood. I slid out and stood as well. We shook hands. I released hers, but she held mine. "There was a time, you know, when I thought that you and Heather might have ..." She shrugged. I told her there was a time when I had thought so myself. "Some things are just not meant to be." She smiled. "Too bad. For us." She squeezed my hand. "Be kind to us. All of us. Aubrey. Heather. Sandra. Me. Aubrey, especially." She released my hand, shouldered her purse, turned and left.

The waitress had picked up our mugs. I was still staring at the door.

"You want anything?" I told her I'd like another coffee. I slid back into my place. I rewound the tape. I pressed the play button and listened. I wanted to make sure it had recorded. There was no problem. It had recorded just fine. I rewound the tape the rest of the way, then put the recorder in my briefcase.

I pulled out my notebook. "Anything else?" The waitress slid the mug in front of me. I shook my head. "Holler, if you change your mind." I told her I'd do that.

I lit a smoke and sipped at my coffee. I stared at the door. Cars were passing by in the main street, people on the sidewalk. People busy taking care of the details of their lives.

As for me, I was watching Aubrey Scott. Flashlight in hand, robe flapping, slippering his way through a snow-dusted night, calling and calling and calling. I could hear the words. I thought of what Marilyn Scott had said, about corners suddenly come upon, people disappearing from view. I thought of the tinge of regret in her voice, having failed to see what was about to happen, what was destined to take place. Futile, of course.

Madness comes, thief in the night, cowardice equalled by cunning and stealth. You never know until too late — a dustless circle on the sideboard shelf, nail exposed on the living-room wall — the breadth and depth and nature of your loss.

"My God." Mother had been standing at the kitchen window. I'd been at the table, doing homework. It was late in the afternoon. October. Our third year on the farm. Our second year with The Boat out there in the yard. "What on earth is he up to, now?"

She knew perfectly well, of course. She knew, without having to ask, that he was altering the shape of our lives, once more, in significant but puzzling patterns.

Where he'd got the string of lights, I didn't know. A used-car lot, maybe. The string was about fifty feet long. Long enough to extend the length of The Boat. Father had nailed an upright to the bow end of the crib, another at the stern. The uprights extended five feet or so above the level of the deck. Father rigged another upright about midway down the length of The Boat. Then he ran the string of lights from the bow to the stern, securing the wire to the tops of the uprights with U-nails. Then he climbed down and stood looking up at his handiwork. He liked what he saw. He was smiling. Then he lit a cigar. Then he went into the workshop. He came out backwards, unrolling an extension cord. Then he bent down and hooked the extension cord to the end of the string of lights. He wound some electrical tape around the junction. Back into the workshop.

We were out on the lawn, now, Mother and Martin and I. We were standing there staring. We didn't know what to say. Or think. Father's voice echoed in the workshop. 'Let there be light!' And lo, there was light. There were several dozen lights, 60 watters. Bow to stern. Father emerged from the workshop. He looked at his lights and then he looked at us. 'What do you think?'

He didn't wait for an answer. He climbed the ladder and strode the deck and then was lost from view, hunkered down in the cockpit. The hammering began. Shortly thereafter, the whine of a saw. Then the hammering again.

It was against the backdrop of hammering and sawing, hammering and sawing, that we went to sleep that night. Mother. Martin. I.

When he'd called it a night, come in from his frenzied labours and gone to sleep, I couldn't guess. I found him, on the couch, fully clothed, arms across his chest, sound asleep, when I came down in the morning.

It was there I would find him, early each morning, until the day Mother left.

6

"Do you think she's alive?"

"Definitely. I definitely do." Deke Millar shut the fridge and came back to the kitchen table. "Sure you don't want one?" I shook my head. "If you change your mind, just say so." He sat down. Twisted the cap off, and raised the bottle.

We were in the kitchen of the house Deke had grown up in. Two storey, brick, maple-shaded, three blocks off Main Street. Last time I'd been here, Deke was living with his mother and his father and his three brothers. Now it was down to his mother and his son. We'd spent the first half hour, going from then to now. Then he'd got himself a beer and wondered why I was doing a story about Heather. I told him. Then asked him if he thought she was still alive. "She's definitely alive."

"Why do you think so?"

"I don't think so. I know so." I put the machine on record. I sat back and let him talk. I'd had a pretty good idea he would, if I could get him started. What you needed to do with a guy like Deke Millar was make him figure that you figured he was central to the story. He was a sucker for The Stroke. Always had been. A sucker for more than that, too, of course.

Deke Millar had married Heather Scott the year they should have been finishing high school. That was it, for school, for the pair of them. It seemed to happen with frequency, back then. The marriage hadn't lasted. It didn't come as much of a surprise to anyone. Least of all Deke and Heather. It was Deke who wound up with the kid. Then he defaulted to his parents. Heather just hit the road. No 'Dear Deke ...' note on the table. Nothing. Come home one evening, there's an empty closet and three empty drawers and the rainy-day stash of ten-dollar bills in the sock drawer is long gone. He and Heather had been living in the basement. His parents had converted the rec room into an apartment. Next thing he heard, Heather was playing a bar band down in the city.

"Even way back then she was always on the edge of cutting loose. You know what I mean?"

I told him, no, I didn't. "With her, it was always the other pasture. Didn't much matter what pasture. Long as it wasn't the one she was in."

When she'd been in school, and living at home, all she'd dreamt of was being out of school and living on her own. "Easy enough. All she had to do was 'forget' to take her pill. Presto." What she hadn't taken into account was that being pregnant wasn't much fun. Neither was giving birth. Neither was waking up at two in the morning to a squawking kid.

Deke had lost touch with her, after that. She'd surface, now and then. Come knocking at the door and ask to see the kid. Spend a nervous, chain-smoking hour or so, then 'goodbye'. She'd call. Usually late at night. Usually drunk. Bar sounds in the background: juke box music, conversations shouted over the music. "She always sounded lonely. Not her words. Between the words. Know what I mean?"

Months would pass. Six. Eight. Deke would just about get to the point where he wasn't thinking of her. Then there'd be another call.

Then she came back. For good. He hadn't known, until he went into The Harmony one day. There she was: order pad, apron, big smile. 'What'll it be?'

Deke had to admit, that threw him. Having her back in town. Knowing that any minute, rounding a corner, walking into a store, going somewhere for a beer, she might be there. With who knows who. Doing who knows what. Unnerving. Plus, he was worried she'd make a move for the boy.

"Alan was fourteen when she came back. I mean, I don't think he'd have recognized her if he bumped into her at the A&P. It's not that I poisoned him on her. Believe me. Whenever he asked, I did my best to put her in a good light. 'Your mother is confused' I'd tell him. 'She's searching for something that will make her happy' I'd tell him. You know what he told me? 'What's the matter with us that we don't make her happy?' What're you gonna say to a kid who says something like that? All I told him was, 'it has nothing to do with you, or me. It wasn't that she didn't like us. Or love us. She just needed to be on her own. She's just one of those rare birds, the ones you see flying solitaire in the sky.'

"Anyway, what worried me was, she might've finally found her mother's instinct. Decided that she wanted Alan to come live with her. I figured, she goes to court, I haven't got a chance. Name me a judge on the planet who won't go for the mother, every time. Swallow some sad line about having a change of heart, wanting another chance. You know Heather. One thing she could always do, eh?, is sing one of those sad country tunes. I figured she did her act in court and that'd be it for me and Alan. And I could just imagine the kind of place she'd call home. Some forty dollar walkup over the ass end of the hardware. What else she gonna get on waitress wages and tips?

"But no. Nothing happened. It was just like it was before she came back to town. A call now and then. Usually when she was plastered. Once every few months she'd turn up. Have a coffee, four or five smokes, then 'well, been great seeing you ....' Away she'd go."

Deke wondered whether I wanted a beer. I told him, no. I had more interviews to do. I'd be asleep in the midst of the first if I had a beer now. "How times change, eh?" He laughed and got up and went to the fridge and got himself another. "There was times we'd be drinking all night and sleep half an hour and go to work and start right in again after work. Days at a time." I told him those days were long gone. At least as far as I was concerned. "Yah. For me too. Unfortunately."

This led us into more talk of the old times: school and football games and fishing weekends. School reunion talk. Then he fell silent, staring at the beer bottle. Then he looked at me. "Strange, eh? She'd been back in town for a year or two. I'd got used to it. Seeing her around. But like I said, we never exchanged more than half a dozen words at a time. And then, this is maybe two months before she disappeared, I was in The Harmony. It was one of those slow days. She brought me a coffee. 'Mind if I join you?' And just like that, she sat down. Took her smokes out of her apron pocket, lights one up, and starts chatting. Chatty as a budgie. I couldn't believe it. I hadn't heard her talk like that since we used to spend all that time in the back seat of my father's car. All her old dream talk.

"It's one of the things I always did like about her, you know. All that talk of what might be. I mean, listen to Heather for half an hour on the subject of what might be, and next thing you know, you're drifting off in dreams yourself. She had that effect on you, eh? With her, anything was possible. Over the horizon, the streets were paved with gold. The trees were dripping diamonds. There was a happy ending to every story. All that crap. And it was crap. But I'm telling you. Get her going, next thing you know you're half believing it yourself. You're half thinking, 'a trip down the road might not be such a bad idea, son'.

"Anyway. She's chatting away, and chatting away. This possibility. That possibility. I look from her to the counter. I tell her the counter at The Harmony don't look like possibility to me. She laughed. 'This is just breathin space.' That's what she said. 'Breathin space.' She says 'as soon as I catch my breath, I'm off again.' 'Off again where?' I says. 'California,' she says. 'California?,' I says. 'Umhmm,' she says. 'Why California,' I says. 'You know me'n California.' I told her 'yah, I know you and California'. She told me once she thought she'd lived in California in a previous life. I thought she was joking. But she hadn't been smiling at the time. 'Only a matter of time,' she says. I says 'what's gonna be so different, once you get to California?' 'Everything,' she says. 'Every fucking thing you can imagine.' I told her she'd better watch out. 'Watch out for what,' she says. 'Fool's Gold,' I says. 'California's loaded with Fool's Gold.' 'Fool's Gold?' she says. She's starin' right at me. She points at the window. 'There's Fool's Gold for you. This whole town is Fool's Gold. Nice house. Nice car. Nice clothes. Nice job. Nice boat. Nice Friday night at the golf course. Nice roll in the hay with someone's wife, or husband. Fool's Gold? Town's choking on Fool's Gold. And they're so fucking dumb they don't even know it.' She looked right at me. And she laughed. 'You oughta know Deke.'

"You figure she went to California?" "No doubt in my mind." "What about the car, then? Why ditch her car. Leave her I.D. behind."

"That's the whole point." Deke finished off his beer and set the bottle on the table. "That's exactly what she wanted to do. That's what she's wanted to do her whole life. Leave her I.D. behind. Step out of one life and into another. For keeps."

"Why?" "Like I been telling you. She was a sucker for the green pasture."

I asked him why that might be. "She was just unhappy. She just hated her whole life. Everything about it."

"Why?" "Fucked if I know. Really. I don't have a clue. Not a clue." I shut the machine and put it away. I stood up and shook his hand and thanked him for his time. He followed me to the door, opened it, followed me out onto the front porch. He told me this must be the strangest story I'd ever heard. I told him it wasn't as strange as he might think.

The year Father bought The Boat, the town was observing its centennial. All kinds of attention was focused on matters long forgotten: the settling of the shore of the bay, the burgeoning, now long dead, lumber industry; the once-thriving shipyards; the Great Fire. Displays of sepiaed photographs were propped in the windows of many of the shops; The Observer ran a weekly series of articles entitled The Way We Were, singing the praises of the pioneers. On the anniversary date, a celebration was to be held in Victoria Park: horse races and baking contests; a display of antique automobiles; a day-long softball tournament and, in the evening, a concert and dance during which the judging would take place for both the beauty pageant and the beard-growing contest.

Father had stopped shaving the day the contest was announced. January that was. In the weeks which followed, stubbled cheeks flourished luxuriantly in places — The Bank, The Jewellery Store, The Pulpit — where propriety had previously permitted nothing more than a well-trimmed moustache.

Father did not win. The day after the judging, all over town, shaved chins re-emerged, highlighted in their paleness by sun-tanned cheeks. Even the people at the edge of acceptance — the gas station attendant, the milk man, the coal man — had shaved and seemed all but embarrassed by their temporary flaunting of the codes of dress and deportment.

But Father refused to shave. He had grown accustomed to his beard, he said. It was a mark of distinction. And though he trimmed it carefully every few days and shaved up to its borders, it eventually hid completely the knot of his tie. 'If you can't see it, why wear it?' And it was then, that autumn, that he began wearing turtleneck sweaters, even to work. 'You'll soon be smoking a pipe.' There was a smile on Mother's face, but not in her voice. 'And writing poems.'

Father did neither, so far as I know, but his beard and sweaters, his corduroy trousers and his walking stick (brass-handled, hickory shafted, picked up for a dollar and a half at a Saturday auction) served to bring the eyes of the town upon him and to make me cross the street and duck into doorways whenever he ambled down the street.

'Your old man gone queer or what?' The boat — stripped to her ribs and standing naked in the yard — hadn't helped matters. Neither had the Ford. Spoke-wheeled, wooden-boxed, it had caught Father's eye and fancy at an auction and much to Martin's dismay and mine, he insisted on driving it to the exclusion of the Buick. 'What next?' Mother seemed to enjoy these quirks hugely, and to miss the point entirely.

There was more involved, then, than the satiation of whim. It seems to me now that having lived his life in patterns imposed upon him, by employers, wife, sons, the town itself, Father had rebelled at long last as everyone does who lives the fraudulent life; rebelled and set out to redefine himself, remake himself according to some old and dulled but still distinct and demanding standard and pattern of his own choosing.

The closer he got to the centre of himself, the further he ventured from us. Even Mother seemed to lose her power over him.

He came in one evening with a box of cigars which he set upon the dining room bureau. It was like a glove thrown down. Mother glanced at it and then at him, but said nothing. 'I am going to have a drink. Join me?' She nodded, he poured. 'Get me some ice, will you?' I got the ice. 'Is there something wrong?' Mother looked at him, and then away. It seemed as though he might make some pronouncement. But he said, simply: 'Nothing's wrong. I just felt like having a drink.'

Mother disliked smoke in the house; would spray air freshener all through it after smoking guests had departed. Thought one drink would lead naturally and disastrously to another. Though Father had smoked and enjoyed an occasional drink, he had long before given up both in the face of Mother's constant comments whenever he reached for one or the other.

'If there's something wrong, a drink won't solve it.'

'There is nothing wrong.' He turned a cool and business-like face toward her. 'I merely felt like a drink.' And he took his seat at the head of the table.

Thereafter, upon his return from work, he poured himself a drink, making one point, and never had a second, making another. After supper, he rose and walked to the bureau and selected a cigar from the box and rolled it between thumb and finger so that its cellophane wrapper crinkled, and then he pulled on the paper tab and unwrapped it and put it in the corner of his mouth.

He made it his habit to lean over the dining room table and light the cigar from the candle nearest him. He would straighten, inhaling, and then stand in a cloud of his own creation. 'Think I'll go for a walk.'

Away he'd go. Thin blue wake.

I can relate, in a paragraph, the way things declined from there. Several months after Father had been let go from The Plant he was hired as a salesman by a firm which had been his competitor. He was on the road, days at a time. Sometimes as long as two weeks. He was not a very clever salesman. Or an entirely convincing one. After an initial spate of sales, 'sympathy sales' he called them, to former customers from his days at The Plant, his success waned. His interest, as well. His road trips became shorter and less frequent. Within a year he was spending more time at home than on the road. He and mother were flint and rock. Sparks flew, generally over money. The lack of it. Mother had found work as a receptionist in an insurance firm. The firm was owned by one of Father's friends. This fact rubbed against the grain of Father's pride, somehow. All the more so because they needed the money she brought in. One thing led to another.

The war of words escalated. Finally, it was worth remarking upon when they passed half an hour together without 'words.' Martin moved out of the house. Not long afterward, just past Christmas, early in the morning after a late-night fight, Mother was gone, as well. Empty drawers, empty closets in lieu of a note. Father and I found ourselves on opposite sides of the kitchen table. 'It's you and me against the world.' He glared at me. 'Unless you want to jump ship, like your brother. And your mother. Go ahead, if you're so inclined. Won't be any skin off my arse.' I went to school and, surprising myself, came home afterward.

Everything had changed. Father had moved all his clothing back up to the room which had once been his and Mother's. He'd moved their double bed into Martin's room, Martin's single bed into their room. He'd moved his desk from the den to the living room. All the living room furniture was in the den and the dining room. The living room was littered with his sailing books and yachting magazines. On the walls, where the paintings had hung, he had nailed his charts. Edge to edge. Charts of all the Great Lakes. Charts of the Caribbean and the West Coast. All the places he intended to sail when The Boat was done and launched.

From that point onward, his life was divided between The Boat and the living room. When he wasn't working on her, he was charting his itinerary. He seemed never to sleep, unless he slept when I was at school.

Each afternoon I picked up our mail from the Post Office at the back of Samson's store. With the exception of the yachting magazines, British, American, Canadian, the mail consisted of bills. Increasingly, bills.

I'd place the pile on the edge of Father's desk. The bills wound up, unopened, in the wicker basket. 'Why don't you do me a favour and get rid of this junk instead of putting it on my desk.' He handed me all the bills. I asked what I was supposed to do with them. 'You're an enterprising lad. You figure it out.'

'Is your Father there?' I got to know most of the voices as soon as they said hello.

They were friendly voices, for the most part. I stopped lying. I told them Father didn't want to talk to them. I told them Father had no job, no money. I told them we were living on welfare. I told them I was sorry, but there wasn't any point in calling, in writing.

'Tell them they can't get blood from a stone.' One day the Buick was gone. 'Dirty sonsofbitches.' They'd come, the repo man and his tow-truck accomplice, and they'd ignored Father's ranting and raving and threats and put the hook to the Buick and towed it, ass-first, out the lane and away. 'In broad daylight. I can't believe my own eyes. I'll tell you this. When the law starts working on the side of thieving conniving bastard tow-truck operator con-men there's something seriously wrong with this fucking world.'

They'd have taken the pickup, if ever Father had left it in one spot long enough. 'Next thing you know they'll be taking the jockey shorts right off you.' Next thing we knew there were three of them at the door. Father had seen them coming. He was up the stairs, two at a time. 'Tell them to go away. Tell them to bugger off. Tell them to go fuck themselves.' The bedroom door slammed.

They were from the bank, they said. I told them I was sorry, but my Father wouldn't talk to them. I told them what he'd told me to tell them. I told them he'd locked himself in his bedroom.

The main man apologized for making me the middle man. I told him there was nothing to be sorry for. I told him I was used to it by now. He told me what to tell my Father. I was to tell my Father that the bank was foreclosing. I was to tell my Father that in exactly thirty days, at exactly midnight on the 30th of the month, they would be back and they would take possession of the house and all its contents, the land and all that was on it. The one who was telling me this then took my hand and turned it palm up and slapped an envelope onto it. 'Make sure you give him this envelope. It's your eviction notice.'

Father wouldn't open the bedroom door. I slid the envelope under it. The envelope came right back out. I told him what the envelope contained. I told him he couldn't ignore what was in it. I slid it back under the door, told him 'we're in deep shit now.'

'We're in no shit whatsoever. And watch your fucking tongue. And tell those thieving sonsofbitches they'll rue the day they ever set foot on my property again.'

The envelope came back out. Ripped in halves.

7

The town has a habit of eating its own. Especially its young. A certain few.

For instance. Ferguson Evans was a year ahead of me in high school. You will know the type: tall, thin, pimply, bookish, bespectacled, effeminate. A caricature. Queenie, we called him. To his face, behind his back. Fergie Evans tried to kill himself. He was in twelfth grade. Here's how it happened.

Queenie had his crushes. Most of the guys he fell for were on the basketball team or the wrestling team or the track team. Most of them did their best to avoid him, at all costs. Particularly if they were in their running gear. Queenie trolled all the games, all the meets. Always hoping for the best, always shuffling home alone. Then his luck took a turn. His target, the last couple of months that year, had been a guy named Harry Cornick. Harry was a grade back. Short, wirey, all muscle and good looks. His shorts and top were always a size too tight. Queenie was at the finish line when Harry came across, second place, winded. It was all Harry could do to keep to his feet. Queenie offered a supportive shoulder. Harry accepted. You could hear them buzz, the entire crowd, as Queenie draped Harry's left arm over his shoulder, put his right arm around Harry. Walked him slowly down the track, then back again toward the finish line. Then they turned and headed back down the track again. Then they stopped. They stood there talking for quite a while.

Then Queenie left. There were catcalls for Harry when he came back over by the stands. He huddled with some of his friends. Six or eight of them. Then he pulled on his sweat pants and his jacket and headed for the gate, far end of the field. Queenie was waiting for him.

That was half the story. The other half you could probably guess. Harry had suggested the washrooms in Harrison Park. The ones back by the tennis courts. Told Queenie they'd better go separately. Said he'd meet him there, half an hour exactly. They checked each other's watches. Queenie was waiting, stall at the far end. Harry said 'you first'. After you've waited as long as Queenie for a moment like that, you don't waste any time. He was standing at attention, shorts and trousers around his ankles, Harry grinning, when the rest of the gang hooped and hollered through the door.

Queenie's mother told the doctors there'd been at least thirty pills in the bottle the last time she'd looked. She'd had the prescription less than a month. There'd been fifty pills to begin with. Now the bottle was empty. She didn't have to tell them she'd found a gin bottle on his bed. They knew that as soon as the ambulance boys rolled him into Emerg.

Queenie was in the hospital that night, the following day, the following night. The day after that he was seen on the side of the highway, straddling his suitcase, jerking his thumb in the direction of the city. Last anyone heard of Queenie Evans.

Queenie's mother came storming across the schoolyard, morning after the incident in the washrooms. She stalked right up to Harry Cornick. Demanded to know who in hell he thought he was, doing a thing like that to her son.

'Hey.' Shrug and smirk. 'It was a joke.' She took care of the smirk. When she left, Harry was picking himself up off the asphalt, nose streaming, snot and blood.

Harry comes from one of the better families. Cornick's Clothing is on Main, near Tenth. It's what passes, in town, for an upscale men's store. It's been in the same family, and in the same two-storey building, since Eighteen something. 'A century of friendly service.' So says the gold leaf on the window. Harry's old man always drove a Caddy, never new, never more than three years old — a convertible if he could get his hands on one. Parked it out behind the store, between the rubbish tins and the fire escape. Anyone touched it, Harry included, there'd be shit to pay. Sundays Harry's old man would tour the town, hours on end, in his almost-new Caddy, cigar jammed in the corner of his smirking mouth. Even Harry had to admit he looked like an asshole. I checked the alley. There was a Caddy out back of Harry's store. Almost new. Four-door. Beige.

Harry Cornick slid off the counter, stubbed his smoke, walked toward me, hand extended. Shook my hand. Wondered where I'd been keeping myself, these last twenty years. Wondered what had finally brought me back home. Knew the answer, of course.

He was a master at this. "Is that a fact? Why're you doing a story about her?"

I explained. We talked for a few minutes. I told him what I was after. "You're asking me? You knew her as well as anyone. Maybe better, eh?"

Still a weasle. Spend ten or fifteen minutes with Harry Cornick, you'd want to deck him. You had to restrain yourself. I asked him, again, about Heather. In the latter years.

"The latter years was just the same as the former years. She never changed. I mean, not substantially. Frills, only. The frills got wilder. The hair got blonder. But underneath, she was the same the day she disappeared as she was back then, Grade 10. She was a shitkicker."

I asked what he meant. He said I ought to know. I'd grown up with her. Taken her out. I told him to make as though I was a stranger. "You were a stranger I wouldn't have said five words to you. Not with that thing on the counter." He nodded at the tape recorder. Looked at me. Looked past me, down the length of the store. Stared at the action out on Main Street.

"You mention stranger." He looked right at me. "That's what she was. You know what I mean? She wasn't born for this town. Didn't fit. She was a city girl. Right from the start. Like The Stork made a mistake, eh? Dropped her down here when he oughta have dropped her in the city somewheres. She just wasn't born to fit into this town. I mean, when she left the first time, was that any surprise? Were you surprised?" I thought it was one of those rhetorical questions. But he was looking right at me. Waiting for an answer. I shook my head. "Yah, well, neither was anyone else. She left back then, I figured that was the end of that. Close the book. And then she come back. Dragged her ass back here like some dog that's had the shit whipped out of it. You coulda seen her." He made a little whistling sound. Shook his head. "You talk about surprised. Why she come back here is anyone's guess. But I can tell you this." He leaned a little closer, elbows on the counter. Lowered his voice. "It was the biggest fucking mistake she ever made. I'll tell ya. She was the proverbial square peg in the round hole. This was definitely not your ideal fit. She definitely did not belong. What I still can't figure is why she did come back. I mean it was obvious, eh?, she didn't like the place. It was like she was sneering at it, all the time. At it. At us. She didn't make the slightest effort to fit in. She just didn't give a fuck. You could tell." He sat up. He was looking past me, again, down the length of the store.

"Big city woman. And brother, didn't she lay it on. Toronto this. Montreal that. 'When I was down in L.A.' 'Now, in New York they ....' It was like she was going out of her way to piss everyone off. Know what I mean? Like she was way above us. It was like she had her nose in the air. Couldn't stand the smell of us or something. Arrogant. But what the hell she had to be arrogant about beats me, buddy. She wasn't no better than any of the rest of us. I mean she never exactly made it to the Top Ten, did she? And if you ask me, she never could sing worth shit. I mean, not any better than half a dozen other girls in town. Sally O'Neil. Sandy Procop. Carrie what's-her-name. I mean, any one of them coulda sang rings around her. But, boys, didn't she think she was something?"

He had both his elbows on the counter, hands clasped. He leaned forward, again. Looked me right in the eye again. Like he was going to tell me a secret.

"Take her clothes. Leather jackets and black tights and cowboy boots. Jangly bracelets. Earrings down to her shoulders. Face painted up like a mask. A woman her age? Parade up and down Main Street like some Yonge Street slut. I don't know how her mother and father stood it. The shame of it, I mean. And you take and look at how decent the other one turned out. Married. Kid. Good husband. It was like she was mocking them.

"Mocking us." I asked him what he meant. "I'll tell you what I mean. She turned up in church one Sunday. Dressed like that. Sauntered in about three minutes before the service was to begin. The choir's already in the doorway, ready to come in. Elbows her way between them. Comes jangling her way right up to the front. The very front pew. Right there where everyone could see her. Bold as brass. Bad enough. Then she kneels down. I mean, this is a big production. Kneels down and bows her head and makes like she's praying. And then, as if this ain't bad enough." He leaned still closer. Lowered his voice, again. "I mean, you're not going to fucking believe this. She's kneeling, eh? The choir about to come down the aisle. Everyone's about to stand up and sing the first hymn. And she's still down there on her knees. Still make-believe praying. And then, everyone watching, she spreads her arms. Like this." He spread his arms out straight, on either side. He smiled, and shook his head. "I'm not fucking kidding. Spreads her arms like this. I can't fucking believe what I'm seeing. I hadn't seen it myself, with my own two eyes, if someone'd told me about it, I'd have said 'you're fucking joking'. But it's no fucking joke. Here she is, making like she's Joan of Fucking Arc or something. Five minutes. Ten minutes. Choir came in, everyone stood up, so I couldn't see, myself, eh? But a friend of mine was up in the third row. He said she was like that, all the way through that opening hymn. And then she's at it again, during the communion prayers. Unbelievable. Fucking sacrilegious, you ask me. The minister, Reverend Bowman, you could tell he was right on the edge of throwing her out. Why he didn't is beyond me. I mean, how can you tolerate something like that? And then the end of the service, she gets up and turns to leave. She's smiling at people. Saying hello to people. Like it was just an everyday occurrence for her to be there in the first place, acting like some fucking nutbar. I couldn't believe my fucking eyes. And, of course, everyone's giving her the icy stare, the cold shoulder. Or making like she was invisible. And what's she care? She walks out like nothing was happening. Like everyone was being friendly. Jangles her ass right outta there. Shakes the minister's hand just like someone normal. Sashays her ass down the walk, swings her purse in a big circle, drapes it over her shoulder. Like some hooker, or something." He shook his head. "Unfuckingbelieveable."

"You ask me, she got what she had coming. Nothing more. Nothing less. One way or the other, it's good fucking riddance to a bitch like that."

"Who put you onto Harry Cornick?" Cassandra LeMarre was holding her pen, a fountain pen, an expensive one, parallel to the top of her desk. Expensive desk. She was holding the pen between the thumb and first two fingers of either hand. Rolled it, as he spoke. Back and forth. The way men used to roll cigars. It was one of those automatic actions. She didn't seem to be aware she was doing it. But you couldn't help notice it, if you were sitting on the other side of her desk. It gave off an odour of impatience.

Cassandra LeMarre had turned herself into an entrepreneur. Surprise to me. Back in school I'd have figured her for a teacher, or a librarian. Don't ask me why. Soft edges, maybe. But she'd rubbed off all her soft edges sometime during the past twenty years. She was all business now: a women's clothing store, a car wash, a dry-cleaning shop, a donut franchise, half a stake in a marina. She'd counted them off, one manicured finger at a time, not ten minutes after she'd welomed me in, pointed to the chair I should take. There was a certain ruthlessness in the way she mentioned them. An implied victory in the acquisition of each. And a touch of 'I told you so' as well.

I told her nobody had put me onto Harry Cornick. I told her I remembered Harry from schooldays. Remembered he'd dated Heather, once upon a time. "Who didn't?" I told her I figured that maybe Harry would have an insight. "That'd be historic." I laughed. She didn't. "And?" She arched a brow. I told her Harry Cornick had had lots to say. "As for insights ..." I left it at that. She smiled. "That's Harry. Short on insight. Long on breath." She stopped with the pen. Looked right at me. "Long on motive, too."

Which is the way things get interesting, in a hurry, now and then.

"Mind you, he's not the only one." She swivelled back in her chair, crossed her trousered legs the way a man will do, ankle over the knee. I asked what she meant.

She told me to put my recorder in my pocket. "Notebook too." The long and the short of it was: there were any number of people in town who'd have been delighted to see the last of Heather Scott. Long list, and a varied one.

I asked Cassandra to start at the top, work down. There were at least six wives, that she knew of, personally, who'd have paid for the chance to throw the first shovel of dirt on Heather's coffin. Heather had developed a weakness for husbands on the stray. I asked Cassandra if this had been an active or a passive interest on the part of Heather Scott. "Both." I asked if I'd have known any of the husbands, any of the wives. "Probably all of them." I reminded her that the town had a long and proud history of women playing hopscotch with the husbands of their friends. And vice versa. None had been inclined to murder. She said nobody in the town's long and proud history had had the flair exhibited by Heather Scott. I asked for illustration. Cassandra said the case of a certain young doctor might suffice.

The doctor was in the habit of stopping in The Harmony for coffee, before going to the hospital for his morning rounds. Things had started to get interesting the morning Heather had somehow managed to drop an order of toast in the doctor's lap and had then tried to help him brush away the crumbs. Her clumsiness had not seemed to offend the young doctor. Nor had her efforts to brush away the crumbs. They got to be quite chummy, laughing and joking. "She'd spear him with a quick line. He'd spear her right back." The chumminess had no borders, apparently. It was an orderly who'd noticed Heather perched on the fender of the doctor's Audi out in the parking lot behind the hospital. Broad daylight. By the time the doctor left, half the hospital staff was at the windows overlooking the lot. The doctor had not forgotten his manners: he'd opened the passenger door for her, helped her in, shut it behind her.

I asked Cassandra how it had all ended. She asked me why I thought it had. She was working the pen again.

"Who else was on the list?" Deke Millar. I asked why Deke would make the list. "He was afraid of her." I asked in what way. "Afraid of what she'd do to him." I told her Deke had told me all about that. "Oh?" I told her what he'd said, about his concerns over their son, that Heather might go for custody. "He had more to worry about than that." Such as?

Such as a little business Deke had, a little sideline, these past few years. Everyone knew about it. Even the cops. But knowing about it and nailing him were two different matters. Unless, of course, someone wanted to help out with specifics. Dates, customers, suppliers, deliveries, caches. Facts and figures. "And that Heather, eh? She always had a way with figures."

And then there we were, back at Harry Cornick. Cassandra LeMarre smiled. Thin smile. Sharp edges. "Poor little Harry." I asked her "poor little Harry what?" Harry had had the misfortune of having a very pretty little wife. "Just like a pie crust. Tender and flaky." I asked Cassandra if I knew Harry's wife. "Biblically. Or otherwise?" Same smile. She thought I ought to remember, as I'd dated her myself. "Susanna Wiley ring a bell?" "Susanna?" She shook her head. Once up, once down. "Working both sides of the street?" "Apparently."

I asked for details. Details: There'd been a big affair down at the yacht club.

Some kind of race during the day. Big shore supper and dance that night. Heather was there in the thick of things. Crewing on someone's boat. If there'd been a contest for bikinis with the least material, she'd have won it. A trophy for lack of modesty, she'd have had it on her mantle. "Anyway." One thing led to another. Heather had had "a teensy bit too much to drink. Maybe a gallon over capacity." Had found herself in a dancing mood. She, alone among the others, was still in her bikini. As none of the men had much inclination to dance, what with their wives looking on, Heather'd grabbed the hand of her old friend Susanna Wiley. Nobody had thought much of it at the time. Later, someone went out behind the clubhouse to relieve himself. Had noticed motion. Focused, in the pale light which yellowed down from the dance-room window. Saw Heather and Susanna, in mid-embrace. Neither one wearing a stitch. Next thing you know, this guy had a dozen men over by the window. 'Wait'll you see this, guys.' Then: one, two, three. The guy threw the switch. The yard, and the lovers, were bathed in floodlight. Among the watchers at the window: "our friend Harry".

"Quite a list."

"Isn't it just?"

I asked Cassandra if there were other names on the list. She said there were several others. "But I think you've got the drift of things."

"And is your name on it?" She nodded.

"Top or bottom?"

"Top."

I asked why.

"You're a reporter. Do a little digging."

8

Often, when you are interviewing someone who has witnessed an event, accident, fire, fight, that person will tell you 'it was like it was slow motion' or 'time almost stopped.' I once talked with an old man. He was in his 80s. He told me of the day he watched as his son was run over by a car and killed. The accident had happened right in front of the house in which the man still lived. The accident had occurred when the lad was nine years old. The man had been thirty four. Almost half a century had passed. He said: 'I can see every second of it.'

When I think back to my own night of that kind, I am struck again by the curious slow-motion manner in which the events unfolded.

Father had been surprisingly calm. Surprisingly because for the last month he'd been in a kind of slow rage. Ever since he'd received the letter from the bank. Any chance remark might set him off. You never knew what would do it. And your guess was usually wrong. It wasn't possible to take the high ground with him. I'd mention something innocuous — we'd run out of milk, or did he remember to bring the newspaper from town? — and he'd be raging, room to room. 'Is that all anyone wants to do? Hound me? Hound me? For Jesus Christ's sake. Can't you do anything yourself? Do I have to do every Goddamned thing myself. Did I raise nothing but cripples and morons?' And so on.

For a month, I'd done my best to be in the room where he wasn't. And to move out if he moved in.

But that day, the last day of November, he was as calm as I'd ever seen him. He was in a good mood, at least a good mood for him. He smiled. Once or twice I caught him whistling.

I was busy packing. I'd been at it, box or two at a time, for most of the month. I'd packed up all the good china, the silverware, the photo albums, the books. I'd been taking our belongings, six or eight boxes at a time, to the garage of a friend in town.

All that day, the last day, I'd been packing up the remains, things that couldn't have been moved until the last minute: the kitchen wares, my clothes.

We had supper, just past seven. We'd listened to the news. Empty house resonating with radio words. I'd washed the dishes and dried them and placed them in the last of the kitchen boxes. I carried that box out to the pickup. Slid it under the tarpaulin. Came back in.

'Your clothes?' 'My clothes aren't going anywhere.' I told him I should pack his things and take them to town. I told him that once the bailiff arrived there wouldn't be any . . .''Fuck the bailiff.' I told him once the bailiff arrived, and the cops, most likely ... 'Fuck the cops, too.' I told him it was either move the clothes in boxes, or pick them out of the snow once the bailiff and his boys had finished pitching them out the door. 'Bailiffs don't have a lot of patience, Dad.'

'How about a drink?' The whiskey was on the counter. Along with two glasses.

Father rose and went over to the bottle and unscrewed the cap and poured a couple of fingers of whiskey into each glass. He returned to the table, slid my glass across to me. 'Here's to the bailiff. And the bank. May they enjoy the spoils.'

By the time I returned from town it was past 10. Father was still at the kitchen table. There was an inch of whiskey in the bottom of the bottle. He split it: his glass, my glass.

'I want to tell you something. I may have told you before, or I may not. If I did, it's worth hearing twice. I have made it a policy of mine, a personal policy, to chase dreams. That's what I am. A dreamchaser. I have had only a few dreams in my life. But I have chased them relentlessly. And let me tell you this: the only satisfying moments in my life, and there haven't been many, were those moments of pursuing my dreams. Some cheesy bastard once wrote: 'our dreams are all we own'. Dreadful but true. True as anything you'll ever hear. Let me tell you this: never let any sonofabitching bank or sonofabitching cop or sonofabitching bailiff ever get between you and your dream. They'll all try. The sonsofbitches do nothing else but. Screw them. Capital S. You chase your Goddamned dreams. No matter what. Without them, you know what you've got?' He held up a thumb and forefinger, in the shape of an O. 'Sweet fuckall, my boy. Sweet fuckall.'

It was just past eleven when he drank off the last of the whiskey. Fired the glass at the window over the sink. Missed. Glass shards shimmered in the bare-bulb light.

He lifted his coat down from the hook by the door, struggled an arm into one sleeve, fought with the other, stepped into his boots and stepped out the door. He was still zippering his coat as he crossed the yard. I lit a smoke and watched him go. Tacked left, then right, then left, out to the workshop. A moment later, the lights were dancing in the wind.

A moment after that, Father emerged from the workshop, carrying something. Heavy, apparently. He was off-centre, with the weight of it. He struggled it up the ladder, then climbed back down. Another trip. Another load. Father struggled up the ladder again, and then pulled the ladder up after him, laid it on the deck. Then he disappeared from view, below deck.

The wind howled. The house moaned. Lonely house. A last lone table, two chrome chairs. I nursed my drink. From where I was sitting, I could see the headlights as soon as the car pulled past the windbreak, this side of Samson's store. One car. Then another. Then a third. They were taking their time. They must have been staring at the string of lights strung from bow to stern. They must have wondered what in hell they were getting themselves into. You could almost imagine the conversations.

The cars turned in at the laneway and jounced over the potholes and stopped, one, two, three, just shy of the boat. Doors opened. Men emerged. Two from the first cruiser. One each from the others. The men looked up at the boat. Then at the house. Then at the boat.

They didn't know what to do. They were waiting for some sign which would tell them how this was going to proceed. They didn't have to wait long.

Father's head emerged from the gangway. Just his head. He peered down at the four men standing in the lane.

The bailiff began his spiel. 'As of 12 o'clock midnight, on the 30th day of November, in the year of Our Lord ...'

'You can stuff your eviction notice, bailiff. Lengthwise or sidewise. Makes no difference to me. Put it where the fish don't swim. And then get your arse off my land.'

The bailiff addressed him by name. Formally. Mister ... 'Never mind your Mister this, Mister that. You're on my property and I'll thank you to get off.'

The bailiff explained the intricacies of foreclosure. He explained the shifting of title from one name to another. He began to explain . . .

Father climbed another step. Head and shoulders showing now. 'It's not me who's going anywhere, gentlemen. It's you. And it's right now.' And with this, Father hoisted the rifle which he'd been holding at his side and shouldered it and aimed it at the bailiff. The cops scattered: one opening the door of his cruiser and crouching behind it, the others scurrying under the boat itself.

The bailiff stood his ground. 'Mister ....' The bullet lifted a breath of snow from the yard, five feet or six from where the bailiff stood. The report echoed back, two times, then again, from the rock face of the hills beyond the woods beyond the road.

By the time the echo died, the bailiff was under the boat, with the two cops.

The cop behind the door of the cruiser had his revolver drawn. He was holding it with two hands, the heels of his palms resting on the top of the open door. 'I won't warn you again. Throw the rifle to the ground and come down. Now. I'll count to ten.'

'You'll count shit.' The bullet shattered the cruiser's windshield. The cop hit the ground, then crawled under the cruiser.

'Dad.' Father looked down at me. I was standing in front of the cruiser.

'What do you want?' 'The rifle.' He stared at me, as though not having understood. 'You want my rifle?' 'Throw it down.' 'You want it. You come up and get it.' I walked toward the boat. I put a foot up on the lowermost slat of the cradle. Boosted myself up. Got both hands on the gunwhale.

'Get your fucking hands off my boat.' He was looking right down at me. I was looking right into the barrel of the gun. 'Get your fucking hands off my boat or I'll blow your fucking head off.'

'Dad.' 'Dad nothing.' He put his boot on my right hand. Then his weight. I yelled for him to stop.

He lifted his foot. Then he slammed it down. Full force. The cops tried to catch me. They managed to soften my fall. Then they dragged me into the shelter of the boat.

'I'm giving you three minutes to get your arses in those cars and get the hell off my land. All of you. Every fucking one of you. Starting now.'

We could smell the gasoline before we could see it, trails of it, rivering down from the gutters of the gunwhale railings. We could hear Father working his way forward from the cockpit. Then the empty jerry can bounced off the roof of one of the cruisers. The second can followed the first, a few moments later.

'One minute.' The cops were looking at each other. Then they looked at me.

But it was the bailiff who spoke. 'Will he do it?'

'You're fucking right I'll do it. Twenty seconds.'
'He will.' I was the first out. I backed away from the boat until I was in front of the cruiser. He was in the cockpit. He had the rifle in one hand. Lighter in the other.

'Get your fucking friends into their cars and get them the hell of out of here, sonny. Fucking little sneak. Fucking little spy. Who'd ever have thought? My own fucking son. My own fucking flesh and blood. I should've known. Should've fucking known. Just like your fucking mother, aren't you. Carbon fucking copy of your fucking mother. And your brother. Stab me in the back every chance you get."

The bullet hit a foot to my left. Maybe less than that. 'Get your traitorous ass out of here. Take your cop friends with you. I ever see you again, or your fucking friends, I'll blow your fucking brains out. Ten seconds. Now ....'

The bullet caught him in the shoulder. Spun him half around. The rifle hit the deck. We could hear it rattle. The second bullet caught him in the thigh. It brought him down. The cops, the two who'd been under the boat, were scrambling now, climbing the cradle to get to him.

The last part, the last couple of minutes, it's this part I've got frame by frame.

The cops reaching the gunwhale; climbing aboard; getting Father to his feet.

One of the cops lifting the ladder, then sliding it down to the ground. Testing it.

The other cop, grabbing my father by the arm and getting him to his feet, draping Father's arm around his own shoulder so as to support him to the ladder. Father hopping, and cursing him, the whole way.

Into Thin Air

Then the first cop getting onto the ladder, climbing down a couple of rungs, getting ready to support Father on the climb down.

Father getting turned around, getting his good leg onto the ladder, hopping down a rung, and then another, until his head was level with the gunwhale.

Then the flames raced left and right, simultaneously; raced the length of the deck and flicked high into the darkness.

The cop yelled, the cop below my father, and half slid and half jumped to earth. The other cop, the one on the deck, leapt out into air, arms stretched out to either side, flaming jacket flapping, landed in the snow half a dozen feet from the boat, rolled and rolled until the flames were out, his jacket sizzling.

Father hopped down rung after rung. Two of the cops had him before he hit the ground. Had his hands behind his back, had the handcuffs on him, threw him on his back on the ground. 'Move one fucking inch and I'll blow a hole in your crazy fucking head, asshole.'

'Be my fucking guest.'

It's like I'd said to Deke Millar: a story has got to be pretty strange to impress me. I'm a veteran of the strange ones. Impressed or not, I'm always curious. Always left wanting answers. The question is generally the same. Why did this happen? The answers are as varied as the characters in the stories. No two are ever the same.

Get the answer or you'll drive yourself crazy. Write the answer into your story or your editors will drive you crazy. Stories cry out for answers. It's almost like a voice. You get to a certain spot in the story and you find yourself asking the question. If the answer isn't there, in the very next paragraph, it's like a gaping hole in the story. A hole like that is big enough to drive a truck through. As editors are quick to point out. There are only two explanations for a hole like that in your story. You were too stupid to hear the question. You were too lazy to answer it.

The question nagging me was the one about Heather Scott's green pastures. I needed to find someone who could answer it for me. Someone who'd known Heather Scott well. Maybe grown up with her, stayed close, someone who had been trusted with secrets. Someone with insights.

Deke had given me a couple of names. He didn't know how much they knew, or would tell me. But he said it was worth a try. If anyone knew what was going on inside Heather's head, these two might. They'd been like sisters, way back when. They'd stayed in touch.

Of the two, one wouldn't talk. And she didn't think I should be snooping around the remains of Heather's life 'like some mongrel around the garbage'. Her name was Marni Sanders. I'd never been a big fan of hers, either.

The other one was Teresa Anderson. Terry to her friends. I remembered her, vaguely. She invited me in and we sat in the living room which was one of those designer living rooms. Everything in its place. We talked in a general way about the facts of the case. She said she still wondered what had happened to Heather. Whether she was alive or dead. 'Either way, it doesn't make much difference. Does it?'

I asked what she meant. 'She got what she wanted.' I asked what that might be. 'To be out of the old home town, once and for all.' I told her that's why I'd come. To find out about that. 'Find out about what?' To find out what had driven her from town, what had made her want to always be somewhere other than the place in which she found herself. I told her there had to be some kind of explanation. Maybe something in the way she'd been brought up. Something that had happened between her and her parents. Her and her sister. Her and her lover.

'Who knows?' I told her someone had to know. 'What makes you think so?' I told her everyone knew how unhappy Heather Scott had been, how unsettled. I said there had to be some kind of logical explanation.

'Who says?' I shrugged. I smiled. 'All you're going to get is hunches. Guesses. Gossip. I could give you six hunches of my own. And you haven't mentioned one of them yet. But what's that going to prove? Someone will say it's all because of Heather's mother. And someone else is going to say it's all because of Heather's father. Or her sister. Or her husband. Or an old teacher. Or the preacher. How would they know? They'd be speculating. Nothing more, nothing less. And why would you be interested in writing down someone's idle speculation about Heather's life. What purpose would that serve?'

We sat for a moment, looking at each other. Then I told her all I was trying to do was get to the bottom of things. I told her I had more questions than I had answers. I told her I was like an accountant. Things had to balance. Question, answer. Riddle, explanation. It was a weakness of mine, wanting to know why things turn out the way they do.

'You'll never know.' She was smiling as she said so. A cold thin smile. 'You or anyone else. Nobody knows. Maybe not even Heather herself, if she's still alive. And in the end, does it really matter? You say you're trying to solve a mystery. But what you're really trying to do is point a finger. Assign blame. Assign guilt. To what purpose? Blame and guilt aren't going to bring Heather back from where ever she is. This world or the next. The only thing you'll accomplish is to let yourself off the hook. The old children's ploy. Maybe everyone's on the hook. Maybe the whole town. And maybe no-one's on the hook. Maybe it's like the T-shirt says. Shit happens. It could well be, you know.'

She smiled again. She said I hadn't answered her question. I asked her which question she wanted answered. She said she wanted to know why I wanted to know. Why I wanted to write a story about it.

I told her Heather Scott's story might prove instructive. I told her that reading it might induce others to be kinder to each other, gentler, more loving, more considerate. If the lack of those things had caused her unhappiness in the first place.

"My my." She shook her head ever so slightly. "What a lot of baggage to load on one little story." She stared right at me. Not a friendly pair of eyes. "What's the real reason?"

9

Jenny White closed and locked the door of the pickup box, shouldered her mail bag, started off down the street. "Hope you're in good shape. I don't waste much time." Never had, Jenny White.

She'd been on the track team. She was always finishing in the top ten. Once or twice a year, she'd come in second or third. In her last year, she'd gone all the way: through the regionals and the provincials to the nationals. The Observer had followed her exploits. The stories got longer and more detailed. She won the bronze, overall. Her picture was top of the front page. Four columns by half a page. In our town, heroes were hard to come by. We made the best of the ones we had.

Last I'd heard, she'd gone off to university. I wouldn't have thought she'd be back in town. Certainly not as a letter carrier. "Why not?" I told her I thought she'd have wound up as an instructor at a university, or as a high school gym teacher. She laughed, and headed up someone's walk. "Think I've let the town down?"

When she rejoined me on the sidewalk I told her, no. Not that. I told her I thought she'd have made a great coach. "Who says I'm not?"

As it turned out, she was coaching, as a volunteer. Senior girls, junior girls, at the high school. "Best of all possible worlds. I get to work with the kids. I run the teams. People are grateful. The principal, the other teachers. And they're reluctant to criticize, or meddle with someone who's donating her time. I get to do things exactly the way I want to do them."

She started cutting across lawns. She was right about the pace. I was glad for the pause when she had to go up onto porches to stuff mail in boxes.

"So what do you find so compelling about Heather Scott?" I told her it wasn't so much Heather, as the mystery of her disappearance, which I found compelling. "There's a sad commentary for you." I told her it was a fact of life. Everyone loved a whodunit. "So, who done it?" I told her I was being paid to ask the questions. "Pardon me, Mister Big City Reporter." She laughed, took the porch steps two at a time. Two at a time on the way down, as well. "What's everyone saying?"

I gave her a summary. "Sounds like you've got just about everyone covered. Except the postman." She laughed out loud, shifted her mailbag, headed for another front door. I asked her what she thought. "Why would you want to know what I think?" She glanced at me, out of the corner of her eye. Picked up the pace, just a little. I told her I knew she and Heather had been pals. "Past tense. That was a long while ago." I told her it was that time, a long time ago, that I was interested in. "In what sense?" I told her I wanted to get some sense of what life had been like, in Heather's home. "You oughta know. You practically lived there. For what? A year?" Less than that. "So what's your read?" I told her I was supposed to be conducting the interview. "This is my mail route. I'll set the agenda, if you don't mind." Another laugh. But a thin one.

We crossed the street, angled across the first lawn. She swung her bag off her shoulder, set it on the walk at the base of the porch stairs. Put her left foot up on the second step, re-tied the lace. She looked up at me. "You want me to say what you're thinking. Right? So you can put it in your story, attributed to someone else?" I told her I wasn't following. She did the other lace. "You want me to say it was her mother who drove her away. Mother or father. Right?" She went up the stairs, lifted the lid of the mailbox, dropped the letters in. Closed the lid. Looked down at me.

"Did they?" "What do you think?" I told her I didn't know. "But I think Heather thought they always favoured Sandy."

She did another five houses before she picked up the thread. "I think Heather had a tough time distinguishing between perception and reality." I asked her where the perception had come from. "Heather was very insecure. I don't think she ever thought of herself as very talented, or very smart, or very worthwhile. She always needed a lot of encouragement, lots of attention, lots of reinforcement."

"And didn't get it?" "Funny thing is, she did. I think her parents were really supportive. At least when I was around. They were always praising her. They seemed to be very affectionate toward her. I think they really went out of their way to make sure they treated Heather and Sandy equally. But Heather didn't want to be treated equally. She wanted to be favoured. Needed to be favoured. Needed to be special. The one they fawned over. As I say, she was insecure. Terribly insecure. Just never had a sense of her own worth. It was sad, really." She cut across the street and headed back the way we'd come. "More than sad, actually. It was pathetic. All the dressing up. All the acting up. She was like a little kid. I think she was crying out: 'See me? See me. Somebody, see me.' And it had exactly the opposite effect. People were offended. Put off. Heather went out of her way to be outrageous and only wound up being obnoxious. People saw her coming, they'd give her as wide a berth as they could. She was embarrassing. You'd run into her, all dressed up like a street-walker, ton of makeup, hair bleached and spiked, and you wouldn't know where to look." Jenny stopped, shifted the weight of her mailbag. "I've seen people duck into stores just so they wouldn't have to look. So they wouldn't have to say hello, or stop and talk. I did it myself."

I was trying to write and walk at the same time. We covered another block and a half. We were nearly back where we'd started. She finished the last couple of houses, then put her bag down at the corner. I finished writing the last few things she'd said. About not knowing where to look. About ducking into stores.

"Think she's still alive?" Jenny scratched the back of her head. Looked down at the sidewalk, then up at me.

"Yah. I do." "Think she just wanted a change of address?" "No. I don't think it was that. I think she just wanted people to see her. And I think the only way she could figure out a way for that to happen was to disappear. Pretty awful, when you think about it, isn't it? That you only become visible when you vanish. That people only sit up and take notice, really take notice, once you've evaporated. And even then, they finally notice for all the wrong reasons."

I shivered.

"Someone walk on your grave?"

I hadn't heard that one in years. I flipped the page. I finished writing what she'd just said, about vanishing. Then I looked up at her.

"Do you think she'll turn up again?"

Jenny nodded. She picked up her mailbag. "Sure." She extended her hand and shook mine. "When everyone's forgotten about her. When all the talk's finally died down. When she's tired of being invisible again. She'll come strutting down Main Street. Bigger than life, twice as rude."

"What then?"

"God only knows." She started to walk off. "Then again, maybe She doesn't." She laughed. "Gotta run. Get the route done. My kids'll be waiting for me." She turned to go, then stopped. Looked back at me. "You in town long?" I told her I'd be heading back tomorrow. Day after, at the latest. As soon as I found all the pieces of the puzzle. "How many more pieces you need?"

"One fewer than I did an hour ago."

"You ever get back up this way, give me a call. Maybe we can get together for a beer. Old times sake." I told her I'd do that. She waved, turned, headed down the street.

My handwriting is so bad, I don't type up my notes right after an interview, I'll never make out half of what I've written down. Plus, I use a casual form of shorthand, writing down significant words, leaving out others. Next day, the notebook is in a different language, in a hand I can't decipher. If I start typing within an hour or two, I can still hear the words the person spoke during the interview. Entire quotes. Including the words I'd skipped over in my notes. I've developed a terrific memory. But it's short term.

I drove back to The Pink Flamingo right after I'd said goodbye to Jenny White. Poured myself a drink. Set up the portable on the bed. Lit a smoke. Started hammering away. When I looked up, nearly an hour had passed.

I freshened my drink. Lit another smoke. Pulled all the typewritten notes from the other interviews. Set myself up in the armchair by the window. Feet on the edge of the bed, notes in my lap.

I started back at the notes from my conversations with Aubrey Scott. Worked right through from there. I was looking for some thread which led naturally from one interview to the next. A thread I could follow through all of them to some kind of answer. Some kind of explanation that would make some sense. Plus, I was looking for holes that needed filling. Questions which needed answering.

I put the notes in order and set them in my briefcase. Pulled out a manilla envelope. Inside there was a folded newspaper page and a piece of foolscap, encased in plastic. Unfolded the newspaper page. Spread it on the bed. Looked at Heather's face. It was like one of those portraits you see in an art gallery. Move from side to side and the eyes seem to be following you. Apart from the eyes, I wouldn't have recognized that face as belonging to Heather Scott. She'd put on a lot of hard miles. Fleshed out. Gone the pointy chin, the slightly sunken cheeks, the prominent cheekbones. She was a year or two shy of a double chin. Gone, the long auburn hair. In the picture she was blonde, shorn. Apart from the eyes, brown to the point of blackness, no trace, in this newspaper face, of the girl I'd known.

I leaned back in my chair. Looked at the piece of foolscap. Heather's feathery hand:

> *you enter my mind*
> *through the corner of my eye*
> *and, just as suddenly*
> *- cutting across the quad -*

Into Thin Air

are lost to view
my heart rises
despite itself
full moon in a star-splashed sky
so brilliantly perfect
it brings a tear to the eye
perfectly reflecting
the light of the sun
which has fled beyond the horizon
which bestows heat and light
elsewhere, now, leaving
my heart to bask
in its distant, heatless
glow in this distant, heatless
void

I flip the page.

Where did you come from?
How is it
you found your way
to my doorway
a shimmering, gilt-edged
silhouette, back-lit
by hallway lamp?
How is it you glide
so effortlessly
across my uncomplaining
 floor, sit so
weightlessly
upon my unresponding bed.
How is it your lips,
so soft, so utterly
lack warmth? How is it
your breath, so sweet

is but a draft
upon my cheek? How is it
I open my eyes to this
echoing dark?
Where have you gone?

I thought of Heather. Her eyes. How they flashed.

It's about a ten minute drive from The Pink Flamingo to the high school. I parked on the side street, locked the car. There's an access road that runs behind the school. It runs right along the base of the East Hill. Up top is the house we first moved to, when we moved from the city to the town. As a kid I used to cut down a path from our house to the back of the school. At the base of the path there was an alcove, and a back door to the school. Inside the door, turn left, and you're in the main hallway. My locker was third one down, after you made that left turn. I could leave my house at five to nine and be in class before the bell rang. Even in winter, when I had to get rid of jacket and boots.

In one corner of the alcove there's a dumpster. Didn't use to be. Otherwise, it was the same. Asphalt and barred windows. Graffiti sprayed on the brickwork. 'Fuck Yaeger'. 'Sally G. Goes Down'. 'Bartlett's EZ'. And so on.

We used to slip out here to smoke. You weren't supposed to smoke on school property but they didn't care, as long as they couldn't see you. No one could see you in the alcove unless they were making a point of watching. Smoke and screw around and fight.

It was a spring day, the day I'm thinking of. The kind of day when you hate to be in class. The sky blue enough to make your heart ache, the breeze warm and heavy, flowers and grass. A couple of the guys and I had brought our lunches out. We were sitting on the brick retaining wall at the base of the cliff. We'd finished eating. We were having a smoke. Trying to outdo each other, dirty jokes.

Benny Girard came screaming out the door. He had a sheaf of papers in his hand. He was holding the papers up, like some kind of prize. Hooping and hazooing. That was Benny. A couple more guys came out on the tear, right on his heels. And then one more solitary soldier. Benny started divvying up the sheets. 'Get a load of this one.' 'Wait'll you read this.' They were all laughing and talking a little too loud. 'Hey you assholes. Get over here.' Benny was talking to me, and the guys sitting to either side of me. 'What's up?' It was one of the other guys who answered: 'Benny's scoffed Scott's poetry. C'mere. You gotta read this shit.' He began reading, in a mimicking tone. We got up and joined them. Benny gave us each a sheet. The guy who'd started reading had read himself into hysterics. Another guy picked right up, reading one of Heather's poems. Exaggerating the words. Mocking their content. He was in full flight when Heather came out the door.

She waded right into the centre of the ring of our circle. Walked right up to Benny. Made a grab for the sheaf of pages. He lifted his arm. Then all the arms were up. Pages fluttering.

The guys were laughing. Forced laughter. Raw, harsh. One of the guys was still reading. Then another started. Then another. Heather jumped, trying to reach some of the pages. She was crying.

Crying and yelling for the guy to give her the poems. She went from upraised arm to upraised arm. Screaming, now, and sobbing. Out of control. Eyes streaming. Nostrils bubbled with snot, bubbles bursting, snot and tears running. She came up to the guy next to me. Made a jump for the pages. Missed them, by an inch or less. 'Give me that fucking poem or ...' 'Or what?' She kneed him. He went down in a heap. She grabbed the crumpled poems. Went to the next guy. Left a fingernail trail down the side of his face. Then she turned. Faced me. Stared at me, but made no move to approach me. Looked at my upraised hand, her poems between my fingers and thumb. Then our eyes met. We could not have stood there like that for more than four or five seconds. Already, the others were jumping up and down, taunting her. Mocking her. Calling her names. One of them was right behind her, shredding the pages he held. It seemed, for an instant, she was going to say something to me. But she said nothing. Wiped her running nose with the back of her arm. Wheeled. Found herself face to face with the shredder. Punched him in the crotch. Grabbed the shreds of paper from his hand. 'What a little ballbuster.' Benny waved his pages toward her. 'Wanna bust some real balls?' He moved toward her, shaking the pages. 'Try these ones, baby.' He motioned toward his crotch with his free hand, waving her poems in the other. She lunged toward him. He turned and started running. He looked over his shoulder, laughing. Tossed a page in the air. She stopped to pick it up, then ran after him again. He was throwing the pages, one at a time, as he ran down the lane toward the sidestreet. His laughed echoing in the alcove. 'Let's go.' First one, then two, then all the rest of them were running, now.

Chasing Heather chasing Benny. Pages fluttering up and leafing to earth. A couple of minutes later they were all gone. Beyond seeing, beyong hearing, beyond the far end of the building.

   I spiralled my smoke into the alcove. Got up. Dusted my pants. All the way out to the side street I was looking down to the ground. Remembering those bits of paper. Crumpled white leaves.

   The Harmony hadn't changed. Regulars on the stools at the counters. Kids in the booths. Coffee mugs on the counter. Cokes and fries in the booths.

   I joined the regulars, stool at the far end. I half turned so I was facing the street. I found myself wondering what it must have been like for Heather, to come back to this town after her days on the road. To come face to face with the past. Face to face with faces from her past. Benny's, and the rest. I wondered why she'd want to do something like that. To have been free, to have thrashed free of the line which had held her, like some rainbowed fish and then allow herself to bite, again, and be reeled in.

   It didn't figure. But then no one ever said things had to figure. I left the change on the counter, nodded to the waitress, had a look at the kids in the booths. Tomorrow's middle-agers. Not one of them thinking that far down the line. Not one of them thinking he'll ever wind up back here once he's made the break, headed for the city, for fortune, for fame.

   Next twenty minutes I walked the Main Street. Up one side, back the other. Looking in the store windows. Seeing my reflection. I found myself thinking about the things Jenny White had told me.

About Heather wanting people to see her. About making herself disappear. 'Pretty awful, when you think about it, isn't it? That you only become visible when you vanish.' And I thought about what she'd said after that. About the awful irony. That you get noticed, all right, but for all the wrong reasons.

It was past eight by the time I got back to the motel. I was of two minds. I thought maybe I should pack my gear and head for the city. It wasn't an appealing prospect. It would be two in the morning before I got back to the city. If I stayed the night, got up early, I'd be back by noon. I'd be rested. I could go in and start writing. I'd have my story done by evening. I wanted to go. But there was a nagging silence in the midst of all the voices in my mind. There was something which needed to be addressed. And I couldn't put my finger on it.

I finished the bottle, pondering phantoms. Finished a smoke, shut the light. Next thing I knew it was twenty to twelve, the room alternately pink and black.

Try that some time. Twenty to twelve, Room 6, The Pink Flamingo Motel.

I turned on the TV. John Wayne. Test pattern. Talking heads in front of a map of the world. A bouffant preacher yelling into the camera, his Donation Line telephone number tracking the screen just below his powdered chin. I turned it off. Sat in a chair by the window. Now and then a car, coming back to town, or a truck leaving it. Long stretches when the only motion was the pink flamingo taking one neon step after another, never getting a step closer to whatever destination it was seeking to achieve.

10

We were a few days the far side of a full moon. The sky was cloudless, stars shouldering each other, wink and nod. Just past Samson's store I killed the headlights. Half a mile shy of the home place I aimed for the shoulder, rolled to a stop.

A concert of crickets. Somewhere an owl, elsewhere a dog. I walked down the centre of the road, stopping now and then to crane back and look straight up. Work for balance against the swirl of planets, suns and moons. I wondered how many of those suns had disappeared into darkness, leaving as proof of existence only a centuries-long trail of light hurtling toward extinction. I wondered if, on one of those planets still out there, Neptune, Mars, someone was craning back, hands in pockets, wondering whether on one of those distant planets someone was craning back, hands in pockets, looking at him.

The lights were on in the front room. I turned my back, cupped the match, blew it out, turned, looked at the house again. Peculiar, looking at the farmhouse from this distance. Standing on the road at the edge of property once ours. No longer belonging. But not detached from the place, either. It was like standing on an island, equidistant from two familiar shores.

I turned my back and started up the farmer's lane. Didn't turn again until I was standing on the spot where they'd found Heather's car. Then I sat on the grass, between the tire tracks. I sat right where the car had been.

Yellowed window winking through gently moving branches. It was by that window I'd sat, the morning after the incident with Father. I'd come back from the hospital just before dawn. Night giving way to daylight.

My clothes were stained with Father's blood. I'd undressed in the yard. Shirt, pants, underwear. Stood naked in the pale white light, breath clouding in front of me, shivering. Staring at the charred remains of the boat. I could see Father, yet. On his back, on the ground, hands behind his back, sneering at the cop. Daring him. Pull the trigger. It would not be the last time I'd wonder whether it wouldn't have been kinder to do so. As Henry Hill had foretold, cocking his thumb, aiming his finger. Then I went in, bloodied clothes heaped in the grey-dawn yard.

My closet was empty, all my clothes in a box in the back of the truck. I went to Father's room. Took from his closet shirt and slacks, pulled them on, and went back downstairs. Carried one of the chrome-legged kitchen chairs through the hall and living room to the front window. Sat and waited. Hadn't waited long.

All that morning, the cars came out from town along the Old Shore Road, up The Linden Hill and turned at Hurl Samson's store and came along The Anson Road, slowing as they approached the gate-leaning head of our lane. One or two, not cars I recognized, all but stopped then coasted from view. Out of view they turned in at Henry Hill's lane, reversed into the rutted road and slowly passed again going the way they had come.

You could see the faces close to the windows, first on the driver's side, then on the other. The faces of children still visible in the rear windows as the cars passed beyond the windbreak elms which bordered the western field. Elms dead and long gone now. Dozens of cars idled past in those first few hours as the sun rose and the word spread. Most of the occupants I knew by name or nod. Dozens more were to follow before nightfall, drivers and passengers lured from the calm and quiet of their lives by the news of the night, by the morning's talk of the skeleton with its charcoaled ribs, great gutted bird out there in the yard.

'Goddamned ghoulish.' So someone said, later. But no. It is simply the way we are. News of a death or any other manner of calamity runs through the town and the distict like a kind of low-grade current. You can sense something has happened even before you hear the word yourself; you can tell by the way people gather on the sidewalks uptown or in the lobby of The Post Office or around the cash in the dry goods store; just as you can tell, without hearing the words, by the serious whispery nature of the talk in the booths and along the counter in The Harmony Grill.

It is a fact of our lives that disaster visits most often under cover of darkness. Often, it comes on the highways and backroads outside town, claiming the young. Next morning, The Procession will start: the cars heading out along The Main Street and up the Eastern Hill and out to Saul's Wrecking yard beyond the border of the town. The cars pull in to the tarred and gravelled yard and the older folks simply circle the wreck (Saul always leaving them outside the fence, that first day) and then drive away. But the youngsters get out and look in the smashed windows and so will be able to tell, later, uptown, of the blood on the seats and the dash; of the sneaker wedged between the accelerator and the brake; of the satiny scarf on the floor in the back. Intimations of mortality.

Outsiders are appalled. My cousins, visiting from the city, recoiled the first time I took them out to Saul's. "Gross," they said. And "oh, God." But John Donne's is a felt truth in every small town and township. The smaller the place, the greater our involvement in the lives of others and, thus, the greater our own diminishment at their loss. Having felt a person's presence in our lives, however slightly — familiar face at the cash in some shop or a familiar voice down the counter in The Harmony — we feel their absence, also. Likewise, each person's loss — house or barn — stirs the whole community. Intimately aware as we all are of the difficulty of ekeing an existence out of the factories in the town or off the root and rock rubbled land which surrounds it, we feel keenly for those whom disaster befalls. It is in this spirit, it seems to me, that we circle the wrecks and idle past the ruins: in mourning and in sympathy.

This, also: we are, all of us, checking our pulses. Fearful and trembling beside this sythed spot where one stood, and stands no more.

More than one person coasting past that morning would have remembered Abe Dixon. More than one would have found himself doing that morning precisely what he had done years earlier after Abe's barn had gone up in flames in the night: gear down, third to second, and take his foot off the accelerator and glide past.

There would have been talk, no doubt, in some of those cars of the circularity of Life; of the strange way in which events far in the past come eventually into focus and are seen clearly for the omens they were all along. Talk among people of a certain age.

Among the young, just the shaking of heads. Many years ago, I interviewed a man who had survived a boating tragedy. He and his brother had gone fishing. They were drift fishing. They motored up the river, then turned the boat and cut the engine. Cast. Let their lines run out a hundred feet or more. Allowed themselves to drift down the river very nearly to the lake. Sat and smoked, drank beer until it was time to turn and repeat the process. Just about dusk they were debating the merits of packing it in, or making one last run. They decided the matter with the flip of a coin. Tails. They headed back upriver.

They got to the spot where they usually turned. The survivor's brother was driving the boat. He killed the engine. Then he stood up. He unzipped his fly. Lost his balance.

Of the two, only one could swim and he jumped in, made for his floundering brother. Reached his brother just at that moment when his brother's hands, thrashing for purchase, disappeared in a froth of bubbles. Their fingers had touched. The very tips of their fingers.

What he told me was this: "I knew, then, how the trapeze artist feels. The one hanging by his knees, hands dangling. Watching the other fall. Without a net."

I was sixteen, the summer Heather and I became friends. About to turn seventeen. We spent a lot of our time just driving around. It was the thing to do. Up Main Street and down to Harrison Park. Park, talk. Head back uptown. Park. Gawk. Talk to whoever happened to be passing by on the sidewalk, or in a car.

One night I asked her if she felt like driving out to the township. To look at the moon, and the stars. I remember her laughing. 'That's one way of describing it.'

We drove the last half mile with the lights out. Jounced up the lane. Parked a little farther up the lane than the spot where her car was to be found, years later. If you go up there far enough there is another cut in the fence, another path leading to the fields, and you can turn there so that you are ready to drive out. I turned, and stopped on the plateau. Killed the engine.

We sat and talked for some time. And then she reached over the back of the seat and grabbed the blanket from the back seat. 'You promised moon and stars.'

We walked to the top of the field, found a space between the corn and the fence. Spread the blanket. I sat, legs crossed. She used my ankles as her pillow. Stretched straight out. Crossed her legs at the ankle. Folded her hands over her breast. I told her she looked like a corpse. She hoped she looked like a pretty one, and a romantic one.

What I remember about that night are the long silences which punctuated our conversation.

Silences five minutes long or longer. Between thoughts, between sentences. It was after one of these silences that she wondered whether I dreamed a lot. I told her I guessed I did. But I couldn't often remember my dreams. Not those kinds of dreams. Dreams about your future. Dreams about what you want to do, what you want to be. Those kind.

Sure, I said. Everyone has those kinds of dreams. She asked me about them, and I told her. They were pretty modest dreams, for the most part. I remember telling her I wanted to be a reporter on a big city paper. I wanted to write stories about murder and mayhem. I remember her laughing. And wondering about books. And I remember that we then talked for a very long time about books, about the ones we liked to read and the ones we hoped to write.

I wish I been in the habit, then, of writing a journal each day. I wish I'd gone home that night and stayed up until dawn, or however long it might have taken, to transcribe our conversation. I wonder whether, contained in her words that night, is the missing piece of the puzzle of her disappearance. But journal writing was a habit I developed much later. Perhaps too late. I have only a vague memory of the details of that conversation.

Its essence, though, has stayed with me. Heather wanted to write poetry. She wanted to write as beautifully as Shakespeare. Shakespeare was her hero. I remember laughing out loud when she said so. It was one of the stranger things I'd heard in my seventeen years. She was the only person, apart from Ed Stephens, our English teacher, who seemed to understand Shakespeare, much less revere him.

She talked a lot that night about the plays she liked, particularly, and the poems. I hadn't been aware that Shakespeare wrote poetry. She called me a dunderhead.

I asked her what it was about Shakespeare that she liked so. 'His heart.' I asked her what she meant. She loved the way he wrote about the reasons people did the things they did. She loved the way he could look into people's minds, and into their hearts. 'He had X-ray vision.'

I remember her punctuating that conversation with snippets of the poems she especially loved. I remember that she told me, after each snippet, the name of the poem she was quoting. I have read Shakespeare. And I have often thought I heard vague echoes of our conversation that night. Some of the bits Heather had recited, her head in my lap. But I have never been certain those bits were the ones she spoke.

She told me, then, about the kinds of moments she liked to try to capture, in her own poems. The moment behind the moment, was the way she put it. She talked about a painting she had seen once, in the city. It had seemed, in this painting, that light was coming at the viewer from within the painting, from behind the dominant colours, seeping out of it and into the eye. She said that was what she was trying to achieve in her poems. A sense of a story, the real story, coming out at you between the lines of the story you were reading. Surface and depth. Text and subtext.

I remember her telling me that she drove herself crazy, trying to do that. Stayed up through the night, on occasion, trying to achieve what she had set as her goal.

I asked her to tell me one of her poems. She was staring up at the moon. She told me to look up at it, as well. She wondered if I'd ever thought about walking around up there. Or living there. She wondered if I ever thought very much about what was out there, beyond the moon. Beyond the planets and the stars. Beyond the universe. I didn't know whether it was a question, or a poem. I didn't know what to say. So I said nothing. She looked up at me. 'Well?' I told her I didn't like to think about that kind of thing. I told her it was scary, thinking about the universe. The way it sprawled out into space. I told her it made me feel like a fly on the wall. Or a flea. I told her I felt like I was about to get swatted, or stepped on. And that it wouldn't matter. That nobody would notice. 'There's your poem.' She looked up me. Eyes dancing. Grin upside down. 'You've got the sexiest lips.' She'd reached up and back and traced them. Tip of a finger. 'Kiss me.'

She never did tell me one of her poems. And she never did show me any of her poems. The only two I ever read I have kept, since that day in the alcove behind the school.

She never asked me to return them. She never spoke to me again.

Now and then, looking at the moon, I find myself thinking about Heather Scott. Wondering what became of her. Wondering if, in some distant place or some place near at hand, she is sitting, also, looking at the moon and wondering if I, too, am looking up at our old moon. The old children's game. I wonder whether, one of these times, we won't catch a reflected glimpse of each other, as two people do who stand in a certain relation to each other and to a mirror.

What does she see, in this pocked mirror? One pivotal moment in the alcove? Does that moment still ring? Do her ears fill with the sound of it, her eyes with the sight of it. Does she see me still, and only, in my one stunned moment of betrayal. Can she see beyond that moment to all the moments which preceded it. Or is all that — warmth of bodies, intimacy of words, the reaching out of hearts, one to another — blocked from view, from memory?

'My my. What a lot of baggage to load on one little story.' Maybe. But who's to tell how significant certain moments can be. Who is to tell whether this moment, like a boulder tumbling into a stream, doesn't divert the water in new patterns, and change the course of the river, forever.

'Thinking back, I should have been able to see the turning point. That moment when I might have helped.'

Shouldn't we all? It's so painfully clear, from a distance. From this distance I can see, precisely, the moment at which all these lives were altered, for better or for worse: Heather's, her parents', my parents', Martin's, Suzie's, mine.

I could give you the catalogue. I can put my finger on the maps of these lives and say: here.

Here is where the wrong turn was taken. Here is where they began to pick up speed, on the downhill roll.

Yah. But I'm a day late and a dime short. They're all in the past tense now.

I remember the look in Heather's eyes that day in the alcove behind the school. And I think of those two brothers floundering in the river. That startled disbelieving look just before those dark surprised eyes slipped from view. Same look. Same eyes.

Maybe Terry Andersen is right. Maybe fault is beside the point. Maybe these things just happen.

Like drowning men and trapeze artists, we reach out, sometimes, and miss. No malice in our hearts. Perhaps through forgetfulness or carelessness, or some whim of fate, our timing is just off a fraction of a second. We reach out and grab a handful of water, or thin air.

It's been known to happen. 'You've always been there to hold her hand, to make sure her feet don't slip out from under her. To catch her, if they do.'

I could hear Aubrey's reed-thin voice, but what I was seeing was Ben, hanging from my hand, feet skittering above the ice-covered sidewalk.

I got to my feet. Dropped my cigarette and ground it into the earth. Brushed the seat of my pants and headed for the road.

The farmhouse was in darkness. Its roof silvered with moonlight. I stood there looking at it for another moment, then turned and headed down the road toward my car.

"Do you know what time it is?"

I checked my watch. I told her it was quarter to one.

"Yah. And it's quarter to one here, too. And I have to get up at six to get ready for work. This better be good."

I told her I was heading out. I told her I'd be in the city by six thirty, quarter to seven. Maybe earlier. Certainly no later. I told her to tell Ben I'd pick him up. Seven. Seven fifteen the latest. Buy him breakfast, then take him to school.

'Don't make a promise you can't keep.'

I told her I'd be there. She could take that to the bank.

There was a pause. Like she was trying to figure out what was going on. Then she said goodbye. Then she added my name. Her voice rising, through the last syllable, into a question mark.

The Author

Paul Vasey is a novelist and broadcaster living in Windsor, Ontario. He worked for newspapers for 25 years, and for the past five years has been host of the CBC morning program in Windsor. He has won numerous newspaper awards, including a Southam Fellowship for Journalists. This is his seventh book.